ALPHA'S REVENGE

RENEE ROSE
LEE SAVINO

Midnight
ROMANCE

WANT FREE BOOKS?

Rafe

Moonlight glints off the black surface of Lake Como. The villas and their private estates are all silent as I slink past cypress trees and neatly trimmed boxwoods to my destination.

"Alpha One, are you in position?" Channing's voice is a whisper in my earpiece.

"Not yet," I mutter into the tiny microphone transmitter embedded in my collar. I'm wearing nothing but a stretchy black bodysuit that will allow me to shift into a wolf if I need to. If all goes to plan, I won't need to.

In the meantime, I look like a cat burglar. Which is appropriate. Tonight I'm a thief, and the target is the eighteenth century villa built into the side of the mountain.

Gabriel Dieter's Italian mansion has layers of security. The first is its location in a secluded section of Lake Como. There's only one road in and out, and it's heavily guarded. But the guards are human, and somehow Colonel Johnson, the shifter commander who greenlit this op, learned their nightly route. I have two minutes to give them the slip and get down to the lake water. I already bypassed the guards, so now it's time for me to swim.

The lake laps at the rocks, a gentle lullaby greeting me. I slip into the water and grit my teeth against the chill. My wolf doesn't really like the water. Werewolves are heavy and swimming isn't easy. I swim in smooth strokes and keep to the shallows until the walled fortress of Dieter's home is ahead. When I take to land again, I give myself a good shake and fling the water off me like a wolf. I've yet to find a more efficient way to dry off.

"Approaching the house," I breathe into my comm. I take a running leap and twist as I clear the top of the wall. I land silently on my feet.

"Do we need the diversion?" Channing asks.

"No." A disturbance at the border of Dieter's land would draw guards, but result in more heat. The further I can get without alerting Dieter to a security breach, the better.

"Incoming," Channing mutters in my ear, but I'm already turning. My wolf scented the new arrivals: thick-bodied guard dogs racing my way. Rottweilers. I let out a growl and bare my teeth, letting my wolf greet them. The dogs stop in their tracks, realizing they've met a bigger predator. Something about my alpha presence makes their primal senses overwhelm their training. Challenging and soothing them all at the same time. They tilt their heads to show their necks and shy away when I stride forward.

I lope across the dark lawn to the house. There are no motion sensors in this area, probably because they don't want them tripped by the dogs. *Mistake.* I circle the house until I'm below the shining glass addition to the villa, the one modern touch in the centuries old architecture. Gabriel Dieter's office.

I find toeholds in the stone wall and scale the sheer face

ALPHA'S REVENGE

of the house until I'm on the roof. Here, I can make my way closer to the glass cupola. "Almost in," I report. I have a glass cutter attached to my belt, but as I creep along the tiled roof, I spy an open window in one of the eighteenth-century towers. I scale the turret, climbing blind with my fingers searching painstakingly for holds. A breeze rises off the lake and chills my exposed skin. At last, I hug the stone, having climbed level with the open window. I push the ancient glass very carefully. Sure enough, it's unlatched.

Unbelievable.

I slip through the open window and step into a hall. "I'm in."

Trepidation trickles up my spine as I pad through the hall towards Dieter's office. Dieter is a paranoid sono-fabitch. According to our reports, he sleeps in a safe room every night. His preferred home base is a fortress in the Swiss Alps. We tried spying on him there, but somehow he found out and sicced a small army on us. Since then, he's gone underground, hiding in a hole too deep for even Colonel Johnson's sources to find. Until last week, when we got reports of him staying here, in his Lake Como residence. This place isn't as secure as his mountain chalet, but it's belonged to his family for centuries. He must have arranged to meet someone here—probably a warlord or terrorist leader or similar customer hoping to buy Dieter's illegal arms.

I push my wolf's unease away. The only thing bigger than Dieter's paranoia is his conceit. He probably wanted to meet his customers here to impress them. This hallway is lined with priceless artifacts, enough to fill a small museum. I creep past giant gilt framed paintings, Greek statues, a Ming vase. This guy hoards treasure like a dragon. Who knows what other valuables are locked in the vaults below this house?

3

My mission is simple. Break into Dieter's office, grab the evidence of his next arms deal, plant a few bugs. The best time to do this is when he's in his house, thinking he's safe, thinking all is well.

I halt in the hall before the office door, listening for any incoming guards. Dieter's security is excellent, but it's not enough to deter a werewolf. My heightened hearing, night vision and sense of smell give me the advantage.

"I'm at the office," I murmur to my comm. "There's no sign of extra security." No fingerprint or eye scanner, nothing. I put my hand on the latch, and it opens smoothly. "Door's unlocked."

"Noted. Security cams quiet. Proceed with caution," a new voice chimes in. Lance, from the safety of his new home. He's grounded from missions until further notice, but he insisted on being radio backup.

The door creaks a little as it completes its arc, but the house remains silent. Somewhere in the house, Gabriel Dieter is asleep in his safe room. If it all goes well, it won't be until he awakes in the morning that he'll know anything is gone.

The way before me is filled with red lasers. A hundred of them, crisscrossing the entire room. No wonder the door wasn't locked. No human thief could weave through this labyrinth.

But I'm not human.

I back up in the hall and take a running leap. In a maneuver I've practiced for weeks on end, I sail head first over the lasers, high enough to brush the ceiling. My jump ends in a roll that deposits me behind the giant desk. I land close to the wall and freeze, every muscle tensed. Silence. Behind me, the red forest of lasers remains untripped. Two feet to my right is a small safe on a ledge built into the wall.

I did it. "I'm at the safe."

"Roger that," Lance murmurs.

I sidle over to the safe and turn on the special black-light built into the collar of my bodysuit. When I move the light over the safe's keypad, Dieter's fingerprints show up as blue and purple smudges on the keypad. I read off the relevant numbers to Lance.

"There are no papers left out on the desk?"

"No."

The lights in the office cut on. I whirl, blinking against the sudden brightness.

"Welcome, Rafe Lightfoot, to my home."

Gabriel Dieter sits in the corner, lounging in an antique-looking chair that's probably as old as the house. The bastard's wearing an honest-to-God dressing gown. Red velvet, with black silk slacks and beaded slippers. Not everyone can pull off a Hugh Hefner look, but Dieter's going for it. He has thick black hair and bronze skin, and the arrogance of a movie star.

The bastard is wearing sunglasses. Inside. At night.

The lasers have disappeared. One leap, and I could have my teeth at his neck. Except he's holding a gun with an elongated black barrel. "I wouldn't if I were you," he says in smooth, unaccented English.

My comm comes alive with a sudden crackle. "There are lights on in the office."

"Hello, Lance," Dieter calls from across the room. There's no way he could've picked up my comm unless he had shifter hearing, so he must have made a lucky guess. I remain still and watchful, weighing my options.

"Took you long enough to get here," Gabriel drawls. "I practically rolled out a red carpet." He cocks his head to the side. "Did you kill my dogs?"

"No."

He tsks. "So hard to find good help these days."

"I drugged them," I lie. "It should've worn off by now." I won't have Dieter kill his dogs, thinking they're worthless. I spread my hands to distract him. "So you caught me. Now what?" If he shoots me, it'll hurt, but I should be able to escape. A few bullets won't take down a shifter.

"Now I teach you a lesson. I knew you would escalate after your little spy operation in Switzerland, but this breaking and entering is a bit too far."

"Did you think you could sell AK-47s to warlords, and we wouldn't do anything about it?"

"Hmm," he pretends to ponder this. "I wonder what I could give you to drop this little crusade?"

I stifle the growl that rises from my chest. "Nothing."

"Money, gold, jewels—"

"Not a chance," I interrupt.

"The names of those who killed your family?"

My muscles turn to stone. "What do you know about that?" My voice comes out hoarse.

"You'd be surprised by how much I know about you, Rafe Lightfoot. I know you and your brother Lance were orphaned as teenagers. I know you want revenge."

My head's reeling from this when he adds, "Oh, and congratulations. I hear your brother has gotten a human female with child." Dieter's lips draw back in a slow smile. It's the creepiest thing I've ever seen. "Perhaps I should pay a visit."

My snarl bursts out before I can stop it. "You leave him alone."

"Perhaps that's what I'll give you." Dieter says with a crocodile-like grin. "If you leave me alone then I'll return the favor."

"I don't respond well to threats," I say, my voice thick with fury.

"Enough. I've tolerated you for some time. How would you like waking up in the middle of the night to greet an uninvited guest?" He leans forward. "How secure is your little lodge near Wolf Mountain?"

I turn my head and speak into my comm, "Get eyes on Lance, now."

"Roger that." Channing says. "Mission aborted. Pickup in thirty."

In the distance, I hear the sound of a helicopter. My ride's almost here.

I spread my lips wide and show my teeth in my own wolfy grin. From the look on Dieter's face, my smile is as disturbing as his. "Well, this has been fun, but I got to go." I fake towards the window to my right.

Shots ring out, and I dip left, ripping the safe from the wall. Above my head, glass shatters. I raise the safe above my head, shielding myself from the rain of glass shards. Dieter howls.

"Somebody order takeout?" Channing hollers from above and cackles like a psycho. The helicopter hovers over the broken glass dome. I leap and catch the ladder waiting for me, cradling the safe to my chest. Channing's just above me. We both climb up to the bird. Channing makes great time, but I'm struggling with the unwieldy weight of the safe.

More gunshots ring out, piercing the night. Below, Dieter stands in the glass-strewn wreck of his office. His sunglasses have fallen off, and his face is a mask of fury as he fires the gun at me.

Bullets slam into me, almost wrenching my hold from the webbing ladder. Fire explodes in my body, followed by a supernova of pain. I drop the safe.

"Fuck, no!" I shout.

"Hang on, Sarge," Lance's voice hammers into my ear.

7

"He's been hit! Fly, fly, fly," Channing screams at Teddy, our pilot. The helicopter swoops away. Cold air rushes around me as we fly across the lake. I grit my teeth and hang on.

"I got you," Channing shouts to me and starts to pull the ladder in. My vision swims, and my head floats above the throbbing agony of my body. The seconds turn into years. Finally, Channing grabs my arms. I bite back a roar and move my frozen limbs to help him drag me into the bird.

My body is weirdly numb. All I can do is collapse on the floor of the chopper, gasping.

"Fucker knew we were coming," I report as Channing helps me lie flat and rips open my suit to reveal bloody bullet wounds in my chest. "He shot me."

"No shit, Sherlock," Channing rumbles. He reaches for a bullet and hisses, snatching his hand away. "Silver."

White fire streaks along my ribs. My lips are numb. The poison's moving through my body.

"Fuck," I grit my teeth.

"Fuck," Channing agrees, snapping on gloves. Pain makes me dizzy as he starts to dig into my flesh. We've got to get the bullets out; otherwise, my shifter healing won't kick in, and the silver will poison me slowly but surely.

After a millennia of excruciating pain, Channing's done. "Five bullets," he reports. I hear them clink against each other as he drops them in an evidence bag.

"All's well that ends well, Sarge," Lance says through the comm. His stoic tone tells me he's relieved. "Live to fight another day."

"Damn right." I let my body relax. My body temperature rises as my shifter healing takes over, but after a few minutes I can sit up.

Channing hands me a water bottle, and I thank him.

"Silver bullets," he says and shakes his head. "You know what that means."

"Yeah," I gulp down half the bottle and splash the rest over my face and chest. "Gabriel Dieter knows our secret." Somehow, someway, the arms dealer found out we're shifters. The question is, how?

2

Adele

I stand on the sidewalk in Taos, hands tucked into my coat, and stare mournfully at the front of my shop. The glossy gold letters of the sign read "The Chocolatier" in beautiful curving script. I remember the day when the sign was hung—how proud I felt. How many hours I spent obsessing over my sweet little shop's logo, making sure it was just right.

Now the front display window of The Chocolatier is dark. I never got to go back in after the police finished investigating it for clues to my business partner's death. My landlord put a lock on the door, seizing all my equipment and inventory in the process. Turns out, Bing hadn't been paying the rent. I literally wrote the checks to the landlord each month, but my business partner was tearing them up because he was draining the bank account.

The eviction papers taped to the front door make my stomach riot. I've read them over and over again, and I still can't believe it. I walk over every morning, like I'm going to work, and every time I round the corner by the bank, the sight of my shop, closed and empty, punches me anew.

Four years of work, gone. Done. Over. And I've got nothing but an empty business bank account, a bunch of overdue bills, and a storefront covered in crime scene tape to show for it.

At least I'm not still a suspect in the murder.

"Adele!" Across the street, someone calls my name. Sadie Diaz, one of my best friends, waves and heads my way. I was hoping not to see anyone I know, but Taos is too small for that.

Besides, Sadie is in my posse. We're ride-or-die. And she's adorable today in a bright red pea coat and white scarf decorated with yellow duckies. Her blue winter hat looks like something one of her kindergarten students might have knitted. Do kindergarteners knit? I'm not sure if six-year-olds should be allowed knitting needles, but I'm no expert.

"Hey, you," Sadie says. She pads right up to me and gives me a hug, which I accept. She always smells like sugar cookies.

"Hey, girl," I say. "Out for a walk?"

"Headed to the post office to get some stamps." She turns and regards my storefront solemnly. "Adele, I'm so sorry."

"It's all right." I square my shoulders. I've got my brave face on, but Sadie sees right through it. Sympathy softens her gaze.

"Any word from the police?" She asks.

"No." I shove my hands deeper into my coat pockets and start walking up the street towards the post office. Sadie falls into step beside me. "What are you going to do now?"

"Take some catering jobs," I say lightly. "Keep myself

busy. When the criminal investigation is over, I'll be ready to open again." *I just need ten thousand in back rent. No biggie.*

The winter wind picks up, blowing an old copy of *The Taos News* down the sidewalk past me. I stick my foot out and trap it under my boot. The front page story is all about the tragic tale of Christopher "Bing" Ford, shot dead at age thirty-one. I know the article by heart—I read it before it went to print. The reporter quoted me in paragraph two: "Christopher Ford was a son, brother, business partner and friend. He will be missed." And again in paragraph four: "As part owner of The Chocolatier, I can confirm that I and the workers had no idea our warehouse was part of an illegal drug smuggling ring. We are fully cooperating with the police."

Mémère, you were right. My grandma always told me not to trust a man further than I could throw him.

I pick up the old newspaper and crumple it into a ball and stuff it into the trash can.

Sadie watches me with her eyebrows knotted.

"I'll be fine." I return to loop my arm in hers.

"Of course you will be fine. It just sucks."

"Yeah."

"And it's almost December. I know the gift giving season is big for you."

"It's fine," I wave my hand. "If everything goes well, I'll be able to re-open soon." I don't tell her the chances of things going well are slim to none. I have no money, no access to my shop and the industrial kitchen, and no supplies. The shop was doing well. It was in the black, but Bing embezzled any excess cash we had.

I haven't told my parents. They've been dying to be right about this venture failing.

I grin to keep from grinding my teeth, but I'm not fooling Sadie.

She leans forward to peer at my face. "You sure?"

"If the good Lord wills it and the creek don't rise." Even Mémère's old sayings fail to bring me cheer.

We walk in silence for a while. When we pass the bakery, I wave to the owner, Brooke, who's out sweeping the stoop. She barely nods before scurrying back inside her shop, as if I'm toxic waste and my failure in business is contagious.

When we reach the post office, Sadie turns to face me. "You know if you need anything, you can ask us. Anything at all." She swallows. "I know you'd never ask, but I have some money saved—"

Oh God. I hold up a hand to cut her off. "There's no need for that."

"Adele—"

"I'm serious, Sadie. It's bad, but it's not that bad." I'd rather roll naked over broken glass than take money from my friends.

"I want to help," she says. Sadie's a sweetheart, but surprisingly stubborn. "We all do. Remember when you were short-staffed and got an order for two thousand white chocolate truffles with strawberry cream filling? And it was the night before Valentine's day?"

"Of course I remember. You, Char and Tabitha stayed up all night to help me. And I couldn't afford to pay you, so I made blinis for us every third Sunday of the month for a year." Now I can make blinis in my sleep.

"We got through it," Sadie says firmly. "You've faced challenges before, and you've always beat them."

"Yeah," I say. The winter wind feels like it's cutting through my coat. Sadie's right—I've always fought to keep my business alive. But I'm tired of fighting. It feels like I'm pushing a boulder up the hill over and over again. But instead of a boulder, it's a concrete profiterole.

I tell this to Sadie, and she doesn't laugh. "It doesn't have to be like that. We want to help. If not with money then with our time. You can pay us back with baked goods."

"All right, it's a deal. If I need help, I'll let you know." I squeeze her tight. We make our goodbyes, and I trudge back the way I came. I stop in front of my shop and drink in the sight, then close my eyes and picture the shop the way I want to remember it—with lights on and no crime scene tape and a constant stream of customers flowing through the door. I hear my mémère's advice in my head.

Create an image in your mind of what you want and hold to it, even when things get hard. You will bring what you want into existence if you keep the faith.

"All right, Mémère," I say out loud. "I'm keeping the faith. In the meantime, I need a plan."

I turn away from my shop without looking at it again. This is the last time I'll visit until I'm ready to reopen *The Chocolatier*. I have rent to pay and no money to pay it, so it's time to swallow my pride and start looking for a job to tide me over. I refuse to lose this business and concede my parents were right. I'm a trained chef and entrepreneur. I'd be an asset to any business if I can convince them to hire me in the middle of winter. Taos is a tourist town, and jobs are thin on the ground this time of year.

I do know of one restaurant that's hiring. Too bad it's owned by my nemesis, Rafe Lightfoot. The guy who stepped in to protect me when Bing's enemies came after me thinking I had his drugs or money. He told me that now that the cartel's killed Bing I'm safe, but he insisted on installing security measures in my home and ordering me to use it.

Which is nice, I guess. But still overbearing. But that's Rafe: bossy, arrogant, know-it-all. Former military—his closest friends call him "Sarge." He thinks he can order everyone around. No self-respecting, independent woman would want to work for a guy like that. Driving up to his new restaurant and asking for a job is the last thing I want to do. But it's either that or ask my friends for help.

I sigh and slip into my truck. As Mémère would say, *No one likes the taste of humble pie.*

Rafe

I stand on the large wooden deck outside the repurposed mountain ski lodge that now serves as my pack's headquarters and home. The direct light of the midwinter sun has snow melting in patches. I step carefully from bare patch to patch, avoiding sheets of ice. My feet are bare and so is my chest. I'm dressed in nothing but sweatpants, but I don't feel the cold.

When I reach the railing, I lean against it and relax, drinking in the view. We're in the thick woods, but the previous owner built the deck on a small bluff overlooking the snow-streaked mountain and valley. Overhead is a baby blue sky empty of clouds.

My wolf loves the thick clusters of pine. The sight soothes him. We're safe in these mountains, tucked into the woods. And for this conversation, I want all the reassurance I can get.

"He knew we were coming," I say into my cell phone. "Dieter knew. He was waiting with some sort of special gun. He shot me, and the bullets burned. We sent them to you for testing, but we're pretty sure they are silver."

There's silence on the other end of the line as Colonel Johnson digests this. The wind blows over my ear, and I turn to shield the phone.

"How are you feeling, Sargeant?" the Colonel asks.

"I'm fine." I flex the muscles in my back, feeling traces of soreness but no pain. The cold wind feels good on my bare skin. Shifters can withstand cold better than humans. What's freezing to them can feel good to us. "Channing got the bullets out, and I healed up fast."

"That's good." His gruff tone tells me how worried he was.

I'm not concerned about bullets—not even silver ones. I want to know what Dieter found out about my family.

What could I give you to drop this little crusade? Money, gold, jewels—the names of those who killed your family?

How did he know about my family? Better question: Could he truly give me the means to my revenge? I've been searching for answers my entire life. Does Dieter hold the answers?

"He knows everything, Colonel. He knew we were coming, and he knows we're shifters. He knew who I was right down to my parents' murders. There has to be a leak."

There's a creaking sound as Johnson leans back in his office chair. I can picture him now in his dimly lit office deep in the bowels of the Pentagon. He's one of the highest ranking military officers who's also secretly a shifter. "I was afraid of this," he grunts. "This is why I encouraged you to apply for early discharge. Too many people in the chain of command, too many chances for someone to misplace your file. Too many eyes on the ops."

I smirk. "I thought it was so you could send us on black ops that the military wouldn't touch."

"Stop, boy," he growls. "Not here. Too many ears. Let me find out what I can about Dieter. Sources tell me his wealth is growing, which means his last arms deal was profitable. We're watching the crypto exchange he favors for big trades."

I grimace at the phone. It sounds like Johnson wants to pull us off the mission. "What about surveillance?"

"Absolutely not. No more ops. Not until we have more intel."

A loud growl tears out of my chest. My wolf can't stand the idea of sitting around while the trail goes cold. Especially after what Dieter said about my family. "Sir—"

"That's an order," Johnson interrupts.

I don't remind him that I don't have to follow his orders anymore. He's the client, not my commanding officer.

As if he guesses at my thoughts, he says, "Do not engage him. I'm serious, Sergeant."

I bare my teeth at the blue sky. Pissing off Colonel Johnson by doing it anyway would probably be futile. Dieter is wealthy enough to fund his own private militia. The only time we've gotten close is because he let us. What a galling thought.

"I know you want to take him down. No one wants that more than I do," Johnson adds quietly.

I blow out a breath that turns to smoke in the frigid air. "Yes, sir." As much as I hate it, lying low is the best way to keep my pack safe. I won't risk them on a suicide mission.

The best thing to do is to keep us all close together in Taos. My wolf is already going crazy trying to look after my fellow wolf shifters plus their fragile human mates. Not only do I feel responsible for the safety of Charlie and Sadie, but also the women in their close circle of friends. Like their beautiful friend Adele. She's not pack, I shouldn't care about her problems, but for some reason I dropped everything to help her through her recent troubles. Now that cartel has backed off, I'm breathing a little easier. But why did I care in the first place?

Expanding the pack is making me crazy.

I say to the Colonel, "Keep me posted."

"Will do. Watch your back, son."

I hang up and stretch. The movement pulls on my muscles and slight twinges radiate from the spots where the bullets sank into me. Soon the wounds will be fully healed, leaving only a bitter memory of meeting Dieter. I intend to never forget what he did to me nor the threat he made against my brother and his unborn pup. He's not just a threat to me but every shifter.

Just like my parent's murderers.

I won't rest until all of them–Dieter, the ones who killed my family–are dead. It's all I live for.

I head back inside, pausing in the open door to let the fresh air in. There was another reason I stepped out onto the deck to talk to the Colonel. Channing tried to cook again, and the kitchen stinks like burned broccoli. The charred scent was thick enough to make my wolf gag.

The stench lingers. To a human, the scent would be faint and fading. To a shifter, it's like a punch in the nose.

As I walk inside, Lance wanders out of the comm room. He's living now with his mate, Charlie, but still works for Black Wolf Security during the day when he's not in wolf form and stalking his mate on her mail route.

My little bro raises his chin in hello and gets a whiff off the burned food.

"Gawd, that's awful." Lance presses a forearm to his face.

"It's not that bad," Channing grumbles.

Lance points at him. "The United Nations called. The next time you cook, they're charging you with war crimes."

Deke raises a hand. "I'll testify at the trial." The

normally stoic wolf wears a blank expression, but the fact that he's even cracking a joke is a sign of how his mate Sadie has changed him.

"Har, har, very funny." Channing flips them both off. "If you don't want me in the kitchen, why don't you cook?"

"I had KP duty last week," Deke says.

Channing crosses his arms over his chest. "Yeah, and you fed us bacon and eggs five days straight."

"Mmm," Lance smacks his lips. "Breakfast for dinner. Brinner."

"My wolf can't handle that shit," Channing says. "I need variety. I have a very sensitive palate."

"Your wolf went dumpster diving and ate garbage last time we went on a run," Lance retorts, and Channing lunges for him.

Deke grabs Channing before he gets too far, and I stop Lance with a barked order, "Enough! I just got off the phone with the Colonel."

The relaxed, playful manner of the three soldiers falls away as they pivot to face me.

"What did he say?" Lance asks, no trace of his earlier joking smirk.

"Johnson's still looking into the leak," I say. "In the meantime, we're grounded."

"What?" the pack explodes. "What about Dieter?"

"Sidelined until further notice. Absolutely no freelancing. Johnson made that clear."

Channing curses and kicks the kitchen trash can. Not a hard kick, but he's a wolf, so the metal canister goes flying.

Deke catches it and frowns at the dent in its side.

"Aww, Channing," Lance groans. "That's the third one this month."

"Sorry. This sucks." With his ruffled hair and scowl,

Channing looks like a three-year-old denied a lollipop. But I get the feeling.

"It does suck," I say. "I'd love nothing more than to greenlight an op. Kick down Dieter's door and bring him in. But we still don't know why or where Dieter got those silver bullets. We gotta play the long game."

There's a little more grumbling, but I know they get the message. I clear my throat. "Another thing. We're on lockdown, starting now. No one comes in or out of HQ without my leave."

Lance perks up at this. His wolf's in protective mode because he and his mate are expecting a child. "What's the threat?"

"Dieter knew about you," I tell him. I was holding this information back because he had enough going on with trying to get his mate back. "And our family, our past. He asked me if I wanted revenge."

Lance whirls and kicks the trashcan Deke just set down. The container goes banging down the hall. It's hell on the floor, but it makes a satisfying sound.

"Do we need to move our mates in here?" Deke asks. His whole body is tense. He looks like he's ready to run out the front door and head to Sadie's townhouse ASAP.

"Not at this junction. If I get more intel, you'll be the first to know. For now, just notify me if you're coming or going. Keep your phone on at all times. And no visitors. Obviously, your mates are still welcome." I glance at Lance and Deke.

I still can't get used to the idea of half our pack having mates. We went from a light, tight team of soldiers to… something very different. More pack-like. More like a family, which makes my wolf nearly crazy with the need to protect the weaker, fragile members—two human females and an unborn pup. I mean, fuck, what if it had been

Lance who was shot with silver and what if he hadn't made it? He would have orphaned the child he hasn't even met.

Unthinkable. But I have to think about it and plan for everything. It's my job, my role. It's what makes me an Alpha.

"No more murdering vegetables," I say to Channing. "I'll pick up something from the Grille." The biggest perk of owning a restaurant— free takeout. And now we can buy steak and beer wholesale.

"What do we eat tomorrow?" Deke asks. He's retrieved the metal trash can, which is now so dented up, it's useless.

"I'll figure it out." I beckon for him to toss me the trash can, and when he does, I catch it and crumple it into a ball. Not the most elegant use of my shifter strength, but it's satisfying. I pretend the metal is Gabriel Dieter's head.

When I'm done, the trash can is a whorl of twisted metal, good for nothing except maybe to be used as a nice, heavy paperweight.

"I could try bacon and eggs," Channing is musing.

I throw the crumbled ball at his head. He catches it easily, and I point a stern finger at him. "No more cooking, soldier. Nothing but toast. That's an order."

3

Adele

I pull up at the Grille and angle my rearview mirror to put some lipgloss on. Rafe Lightfoot may get under my skin with his drill sergeant confidence and manner, but I've caught him looking me up and down on the nights my girl squad goes out with his crew. I've checked his tight ass out plenty of times. There's a little sizzle between us on the rare occasions our eyes meet. We can't stand each other, but we have chemistry. And I guess if I'm sinking low enough to ask him for a job, I might as well use the only weapon I have left.

I jump out of my old pickup and rearrange my scarf against the cold wind blowing down from Taos Mountain. Inside the Grille, a twenty-something blonde with that hippie-granola-Taos look calls out, "Welcome, I'll be right with you," as she buzzes into the kitchen. The dinner crowd is just starting to gather—half the tables are full for the casual burger and fries fare the Grille has to offer.

Ugh. This is so not my scene—not that I'm judging it. I love a good burger. But Rafe doesn't need a chef, he needs a line cook. I don't know why he even hinted at me working here.

Unless he just wants a chance to give me orders. The big, domineering jerk.

This isn't going to work. I pivot in my high heeled boots to exit and run right into a big barrel chest.

"Adele." Rafe catches my elbows to steady me as I bounce off his immovable form.

I'm more flustered than a misstep calls for, but it's only because my nerves were already ragged over asking Rafe for a job, and now that I've decided I don't actually want the job, I feel somehow caught.

"Rafe," I manage to say. *Don't be nervous. Imagine him naked.*

Trouble is, I imagine Rafe naked far too much.

He's still holding my elbows, standing far too close. Rafe's not as Hollywood good-looking as his brother Lance, who recently knocked up my friend Charlie. His hair is darker. His eyes are green. Lance is charming in that laidback, lazy smile kind of way. Rafe is the opposite. No charm. Definitely not laidback. There's a ruggedness and ferocity about him that makes being around him feel terribly dangerous.

Dangerous, intense, and… exciting.

He's the kind of guy you'd want on your side, not against it. Last week, when my business partner turned up dead, Charlie got kidnapped, and I was picked up by the police for questioning, I learned exactly how powerful it is to have a guy like him in my court.

So I'm already beholden to Rafe.

Something I hate. *Don't trust a man …*

"I—um—I was just leaving."

"You were?" His brows go down, gaze sweeps over me.

24

"It looks like you just got here." His eyes snag on my high heeled boots. "You walk in the snow in those?"

"Yes?" Why did I make that sound like a question? Something about his surly black brows makes me uncertain. I clear my throat and try again. "Yes, of course."

"You need to be more careful. Those boots aren't good in the snow." And there it is, the most annoying thing about Rafe. He orders everyone around. The fact that he's always in fatigue pants and a gray or army green Henley doesn't lessen his drill sergeant vibe. Neither does the way he stands and looks down on everyone, like a general inspecting his troops and finding us all wanting. I think it's great he had a military career—when I first met him, I thanked him for his service—but he's not the boss of me!

I'm tempted to declare that and stomp my boots like I'm four, but that won't help him take me seriously. Or land me a job.

"Are you meeting someone?" Rafe asks.

"No. Um, yes. Ah—" I shake my head. I'm on the spot here, not sure whether to flee or beg. Neither idea appeals.

Of course, he doesn't make it easy for me. He releases my elbows to put his hands on his hips, like I'm in trouble, and now I have to answer to him.

Screw this. I can't work for him.

"Nothing. Nevermind. I have to go." I try to move past him, but he moves to block my path.

"Hang on a second. Were you here to see me? Or did something happen?" He scans the restaurant with a scowl, as if to identify some mystery offender who was rude to me.

Shoot. Maybe I am supposed to ask him for a job. I mean, here he is, insisting I explain myself.

"Rafe, I—"

At the sound of his name, his gaze snaps back to mine,

locking and honing in. When I nervously lick the lip gloss off my lips, his gaze dips to my mouth. A hungry expression comes over his face.

God, I'm hungry, too. And not for food.

Every time I'm near this guy, a slow thrum of awareness tunes up between my legs. His big body, hard and solid with muscle, his dark hair and eyes... I gaze up at him, and it's all too easy to imagine what it would be like to be underneath him. He'd probably order me, as bossy and dominant *in* bed as he is out.

And wouldn't that be delicious?

No, no, no. I absolutely do not want Rafe, naked and looming over me, telling me what to do. That would be terrible.

Gawd, my panties are soaked. Time to get this conversation back on track. I take a second to remember how much Rafe annoys me and raise my chin.

"Honestly?" I say. "I came to see if you, um, still needed help. You know, in the kitchen. I'm, ah, not going to be able to reopen The Chocolatier at the moment."

Rafe goes still, his brows angled together in concern.

It's way more of a reaction than I expected from him. I don't know what I thought he'd do—blow me off or tell me to fill out an application. But instead, he grabs my hand and draws me further into the Grille. "Come here," he says gruffly.

My heart starts pounding over the hand-holding. It's weird, right? Bosses don't hold their employees' hands. My thoughts jumble and knot.

He leads me to an office in the back, where he lets go of my hand and shuts the door. "Take your coat off." He pulls off his leather bomber.

Typical Rafe—not an invitation, a command.

Part of me wants to defy him just to show him he's not

running this show, but then...he is running this show. And I'm here begging. But even more alarming is the fact that if I want to go toe-to-toe with him over whether my coat stays off or on, how in the hell could I ever work for the guy?

I shrug out of my coat and let him take it and arrange it on the back of the desk chair, over the top of his. He remains standing, and so do I. "So what's going on?" He folds his arms over his massive chest.

I seriously don't know why that makes my nipples pucker inside my sweater. It's not hot. It's bossy and presumptuous and way too alpha male.

Okay, yeah, it's pretty hot. If they had a Special Ops calendar, which of course, they never would—he would be my December. He's in nothing but a short-sleeve t-shirt, so I have a full and glorious view of all the muscles of his arms and chest. I sneak a peek at his abs. Nope, can't see them beneath the shirt. Too bad.

"Listen, I didn't come here to discuss my business problems with you. I just need a job," I tell him with probably a little too much snap in my voice for someone who's asking for a favor.

"Okay." He nods, considering me, but doesn't go on.

"Okay, you'll give me a job?"

He nods again, but it's not a very convincing one, and I'm not sure I like the calculating way he's looking at me.

"I'm all set at the Grille, but we're in need of a private chef up at the lodge." He jerks his thumb in the direction of the mountain.

Private chef. At the lodge. The big beautiful mountain lodge where Rafe lives with his military posse. I've been there to visit a few times because Sadie is dating one of Rafe's crew, Deke. I definitely did not wonder about Rafe's bedroom or whether he slept naked.

A job at the Grille is one thing. I'll see Rafe once in a while, but he won't be my direct supervisor.

"Like a one-time catering job?" I ask. I could handle that.

"No, regular."

Bad idea. It would be impossible to avoid Rafe.

I open my mouth to tell him "no" when he says, "It pays twenty-five hundred a week, and I'd need you to start immediately."

I close my mouth and drop my lifted finger. Damn. Twenty-five hundred a week would get me out of debt quickly. I could make a good faith payment to the landlord after the first week—that should convince him to give me back the keys or at least not to sell off all my inventory.

Now I fold my arms across my chest. And not because my nipples are buzzing. "So my job would be, what? Cooking for you and your squad? How many of you are there?"

Rafe scrubs his hand over his face like it's a sore subject. "Three to five of us, depending on who's over. Lance is moving in with Charlie, but they still come by to eat sometimes. Sadie, too, of course," he says.

The thought of cooking for my friends cheers me. I'm Creole. Cooking is a form of love where I come from.

"All three meals? Lunch and dinner?"

Rafe considers me. His eyes glitter like he loves the idea of having me under his thumb this way.

It makes me want to kick him in the shins. And hiss and spit like a cat. Right before he pins me down across that big, wooden desk and—

Nope. Not happening. Never, ever, ever.

"Lunch and dinner would be sufficient," he says. "You could come in and cook dinner and leave lunch in the refrigerator for us.

"So, once a day, in-home meal prep, cooking and serving. Seven days a week?"

"Four. We like to eat out or order in on some nights."

Four. Maybe this can work. If I could get The Chocolatier back open, I could keep working for Rafe until I get back on my feet. The time commitment wouldn't be too bad if I planned the meals wisely.

"I'd reimburse for the groceries, of course," he continues. "You can bulk order a lot of stuff through the Grille."

I stick out my hand. "Deal."

Rafe's smile is slow and feral. He takes his time reaching out to shake, and when he clasps my hand, electricity races up and down my spine.

"How soon can you start?" He releases my hand and leans a shoulder against the wall, suddenly casual. "I'm here because Channing burned our dinner tonight and stunk up the entire house. Turns out, broccoli stinks even worse when it's charred."

I laugh despite myself, partly because it surprises me to hear Rafe say anything light—not that I know him that well.

"How about tomorrow?" No sense in waiting. I need that money. Badly.

"That sounds good. I'll text you the address."

"Sure, give me your phone, and I'll put my number in."

"Oh, I have it."

When I frown, he adds, "I made sure to get it when things were going down with Charlie."

I make a *hmph* sound. I'm simultaneously annoyed and pleased that Rafe Lightfoot has my number. Honestly, I didn't think I rated high enough in his thoughts to merit that. But then, it goes with his controlling personality.

"Anything I need to know? Allergies? Likes, dislikes?"

29

"We are carnivores through and through. None of that vegetarian shit. We may eat our broccoli—when it's not burned—but we need our meat."

"You need your meat," I repeat dubiously. I mean, I'm not vegetarian either, but this planet is being destroyed by human's meat production. Do we really need meat with every meal? But whatever, he's the boss.

Oh, God.

Rafe Lightfoot is now my boss.

What was I thinking?

Rafe

I follow Adele out of my office, admiring her slender form in her fitted dress. She moves with a feline-like grace. Actually she's very cat-like, this female, which is probably why the two of us don't mix well.

My wolf wants to dominate, and she's ready to scratch my nose.

The truth is, I like the idea of the beautiful spitfire Adele Fabre working for me far too much. The feisty foodie is the farthest thing from my type of female. Not that I have a type. Or time for females. And civilians—aka, humans—are supposed to be off-limits, according to my own rules.

But that rule obviously didn't stick with Deke or my young brother, who both just mated humans—friends of Adele.

After what happened with her business partner and her shop last month, I've been concerned about her. The murder of her partner hasn't been resolved by the police, but it seems obvious it was a drug cartel Bing had mixed himself up in. Now that he's dead, Adele should be safe, but I still don't like it. I would like to tie up those loose ends for her.

I also saw the eviction notice posted on her door and the chains around the handles. I'll bet that's killing her, not that she'd ever let on.

The female is proud. Very proud. Which is why I didn't offer her a loan or help. I basically manufactured the private chef job on the spot, trying to guess how much money she needed and how plausible I could make the position without her catching on. One thing I'm sure of— if she thought she was getting a hand-out, she'd flip me the bird and walk out in a heartbeat.

She marches through the Grille in front of me. The first thing I noticed about Adele—other than her gorgeous scent and her curves under her neat clothes—was that she's a born leader. Among her friends, she takes charge, soothes feelings, acts like a mother hen. She does it so adroitly, they don't even notice. But I do. Because it's something I do naturally too, for my own pack. It's the alpha urge—to lead, to protect. To dominate everyone else.

That's why two alphas in the same room is never a good idea. We'll fight to figure out who's in charge, and in the power struggle, people can get hurt. There are a few people I'll follow—Colonel Johnson being one of them— but never a human.

Adele is human. She can't win a fight with me, no matter how many times she tries.

As if sensing my presence behind her, she whirls, her hazel eyes flashing. "Are you following me?"

"You forgot your coat," I say blandly, holding up the garment for her to step into it.

She extends her hand for it, and I *tsk*. A moment passes as our eyes lock in a power struggle.

Once again, I win. A blush splashes over her brown

cheeks, but she turns and lets me help her into her coat. All manners, that's me. Gotta pretend to be a polite human. The veneer of civilized behavior is the only thing keeping my wolf from scooping her up and carrying her back to my office, where I can strip her naked and bask in her scent.

Instead, I take my time straightening Adele's collar and buttoning her coat for her. Her scent is at peak deliciousness, heated by her anger. It must be torture, taking orders from me.

It's torture to stand in front of her and not be able to touch her soft skin. Her lashes are long and dark, fanning over her flushed cheeks. A brown curl has escaped her fancy updo. I brush it back, and she steps out of reach.

My wolf stirs, ready for the chase. *Down boy.*

"Thank you," she bites out. Damn, she's stunning when she's mad.

"You're welcome," I say, as if I didn't just force another display of my dominance over her. With a hand hovering at her back, I guide her through the restaurant. One of our bartender's eyes snag on Adele's passing form, and it's all I can do to keep myself from leaping over the tables and bar to take him out. I settle for an alpha glare. The bartender catches my gaze and gulps, jerking his head down. Humans recognize a dominant predator, if only subconsciously.

I take a few quick strides to reach the door ahead of Adele and hold it open for her.

"What about you? You don't have a coat," she says as she steps past me.

"I like the cold." Maybe the chill will give my dick the message.

I slow my steps and think of baseball but can only watch Adele dash down the steps in her brown boots, as if in a hurry to get away from me. Her irritation hovers around her in a steamy cloud of peppery scent. My dick is ready to punch out of my fatigues.

What have I done? I just hired Adele as a private chef. That means she's going to be in my life, in my lodge, right in the heart of my territory. Her hands, preparing my food. Her scent getting fucking everywhere, driving me mad. And there's nothing I can do because not only is she human—now she's my employee.

Oh hell.

4

The Stranger

He wandered his vast fortress, admiring his endless treasures on display. A Vermeer painting. A priceless vase from the Ming Dynasty. An original copy of the Keats poem "Ode to a Grecian Urn", nestled among a score of Grecian urns.

The castle was much grander than his former home, but he found himself missing his dwelling of old, where he'd stowed his treasure in haphazard piles and slept among the mountains of burnished gold. Like Ali Baba in the Cave of Wonders, only he was no thief among thieves. He was a king and honored as one.

He's always been solitary. Content in his ways, as long as he had treasures and an army at his beck and call. But now he found himself longing for something more. Not more gold or jewels. Something more priceless. Something more rare.

One thing he'd learned in his long, long life: wealth and power meant nothing without one to share it with. Without the one who would give his life meaning. A female. His female.

She was out there, somewhere. He had an array of sleuths searching for her. What did they call these modern age hunters?

Computer Hackers? They all were searching for the female who woke the sleeping beast and made his heart beat again.

When he found her, the courtship rituals would begin. He would woo her in the manner of his people—with displays of wealth, power, and awesome majesty befitting one such as himself.

He would find her.

But until he did, he must find something to pass the time. A diversion.

A file waited on his desk, marked Rafe Lightfoot. *The former Army Sergeant who'd been sniffing around his precious business dealings. In a world where he had no equal, Lightfoot was the closest thing to a challenge he could find. An enemy who had secrets to match his own.*

It would be amusing to infiltrate Lightfoot's world. Toy with his pack. Destroy his peace, for no other reason than Lightfoot was a worthy adversary.

It was not necessary, but it would do for a brief diversion. What do the kids say in this modern age? It would be ...fun.

He paged through the file until he found a picture of Lightfoot with his pack. As he read the report, he idly scratched an X over the good Sergeant's face. Congratulations, Alpha Wolf, you have my attention.

Let the hunt begin.

∼

Rafe

FIVE HOURS into Adele's work day at the lodge, and it's worse than I imagined.

First came her scent, stealing into my office, snaking around my desk, filling my space. Sweet and subtle, with a bite. There are no windows in my small work space—my office could double as a safe room—and nowhere for the scent to escape to. I can only breathe it in, breath after decadent breath.

Next, the murmuring waves of her voice and laugh. The sound is low and a little bit smoky. And with it comes the final invasion: the image of Adele's heart-shaped face, crowding out all other thoughts. It's so easy to imagine her swaying into my office, pushing into my space. She'd be dressed with her usual casual elegance—in a skirt or a dress, something easy to push up and out of the way. Her soft, dark curls down around her face. Her silvery brown skin and long lashes around her incredible eyes. Her face is perfect—how does she look so perfect all the time? She works so hard.

She came with lunch—a type of Italian sandwich called *muffuletta*. A home-made round of bread stuffed with a dozen layers of meat. Fucking delicious. I hunkered down in my office, pretending to be busy when really I was avoiding the kitchen. Deke brought me lunch on a plate. There was a parsley garnish and everything. The garnish smelled like her.

I ate the shit out of that garnish. First fucking time I ever ate parsley. *No regrets.*

She's still here, in the kitchen, cooking. She's been here for hours, working, and my wolf is going fucking crazy. He wants me to tear out of my office, head to the kitchen, and take a bite out of her.

Not. Gonna. Happen.

Why am I fantasizing about giving a human a mating bite? It's bad enough Lance and Deke took mates. The bigger the pack gets, the harder it is to protect everyone in it.

For a moment, the white paper on my wooden desk blurs. *A cabin in the woods, the door swaying open. My parents lying torn and still on the floor, surrounded by the violent spray of red.*

A harsh tearing sound brings me back. The blank sheet of paper is in shreds.

I grab my phone and text Lance and hold my breath until he texts back. He's fine, his mate is fine. The baby's fine.

I'm going crazy with all these lives to protect.

I clear away the ruined strips of paper then check my messages again. Colonel Johnson ordered me not to contact him until he contacted me. The less we speak the better. I don't want to give our enemies a chance to trace our conversations.

We have a few local security jobs, but I cleared our work schedule to wait on news of when we could make a move on Dieter. It's winter, and work is slow.

I log onto my computer, pay a few bills. *Head down, stay focused.* That's what I gotta do.

Another loud laugh rings out and reaches my door. This time it's Channing. At the first scent of food, he staked out in the kitchen. Even Deke found a reason to hang out nearby. And all afternoon they've been talking, telling jokes, making Adele feel at home. It shouldn't bother me, but it does.

Channing better not be flirting with Adele. I can see him now, grinning like a dumbass at Adele, crowding close to her curvy little body...

The pen in my hand snaps, squirting ink everywhere. *Fuck.* I mop ink off my computer screen with my sleeve. Once the screen is clean, I tear off my stained Henley and toss it in the corner.

A creak in the hallway, and Deke sticks his head in. "Doin' okay, Sarge?"

I grunt back. He nods, as if me sitting shirtless and

surly behind my deck is nothing new. "Adele sent us to wash up. Dinner's ready soon."

I jerk my head in acknowledgement to get him to go away. When he's gone, I sit for a moment, trying to get myself under control. I'm half naked. It'd be nothing to lope to the kitchen and snatch Adele from Channing. Toss her over my shoulder…

Can't. Happen.

I yank open a desk drawer and take out a new Henley. I always have extra shirts and fatigues at hand. Shifters go through a lot of clothes.

I should skip this dinner. But my stomach growls. For the past hour, I've been smelling the spicy scent of something delicious simmering on the stove.

It should be fine. It's not like I want to mark this female. But something about her drives my wolf crazy. My wolf wants me to hunt her, claim her. Take her to bed. Or something. He's never acted like this before.

Since I saw her, I've been fighting the compulsion to be near her. There's no reason for me to be fascinated, and yet I am. She has an elegant presence, but really, she's petite. Her head barely comes to my chin. She's human. Breakable. And yet she stands up to me like an alpha wolf. Always challenging me. She meets my eyes in challenge and can hold my gaze longer than any other human in my life.

It makes my wolf crazy and me hard as a rock all at the same time. I already jerked off thinking of her last night. And now she's right where I want her, in my home. It'd be so easy to scoop her up and carry her up to my bedroom…

No. I push away from the desk. I will not be bested by this. I will be on my best behavior.

Maybe I can get a run in before I have to sit down and watch her smile at the rest of my pack…

"Dinner's almost ready!" Adele cries. "Everyone come to the table!"

A minute later, I'm sitting at the head of the table with Deke and Channing on either side, and Adele's at the foot.

It's important that packs eat together regularly. Pack is family, and my fellow wolves are closer than brothers. It's only the three of us here today, but three shifters can eat enough to feed a platoon. If Adele doesn't understand that now, she will by the end of the meal.

Adele's in the kitchen, wearing an apron over her fancy clothes. She's got high heels and a polka dot dress on, and damn if she doesn't look like some sexy 50s housewife.

"Just give me a minute," she calls from her place at the stove. She's got a ladle and is stirring the contents of the biggest stew pot I've ever seen.

"Take all the time you need," Channing says. "Can't rush perfection."

Suck up.

Channing catches my glower and drops his eyes to his plate. Across from him, Deke is carefully silent, staring at his own empty plate. I feel like the stern patriarch of the most fucked up nuclear family ever.

Adele doesn't notice the sudden silence. "I told you, you didn't have to set a place for me." As she leans over the stove, a dark brown curl falls in her face, and she tucks it behind her ear. She tastes a little out of the ladle and licks her plush lips.

And now I'm hard as a board. I shift my weight in my chair, but nothing makes me more comfortable. "You need to eat." My voice comes out harsh. I need to get control of myself. Adele will think I'm an asshole.

Of course, she probably already does.

Adele acts like I didn't even speak. "I meant to ask, where did you find that beautiful art sculpture?" She points

40

to the coffee table where Channing must have set the crumpled trash can down. "It kinda looks like artsy metal work."

"Rafe made it." Channing smiles, so his dimple flashes.

"Really?" Adele turns to me with an exaggerated look of surprise. She flutters her long lashes and widens her eyes. "I wouldn't have guessed you had such artistic talent."

"Only when he's real mad," Channing says.

"Channing," Deke warns.

"It's all right," I grunt. "Not many people know." Not many people know I have shifter strength that can crumple a metal trash can like it's a paper bag.

"So fascinating," Adele gushes with fake enthusiasm. Maybe she did pick up on the awkward silence, and now she's trying to fill it. It is her first day on the job. "I've never seen a metal sculpture quite like that. Very interesting technique. I'd love to see your workshop."

"We'll show you anything you like." Channing bobs his head and grins, kicking his legs under the table like he's five.

"Thank you, Channing." Adele shoots him a quick smile.

"Sarge," Deke mutters, and I realize I've been gripping my fork so hard, I've bent it. I quickly straighten it before Adele comes to the table.

"Here we go." She sets down a platter of rice and another of homemade cornbread. "Fill your plates with this, and I'll dish out the red beans." She hurries back to the kitchen to a huge stew pot.

"I've never seen a pot so big." Channing leaps up. "Let me help you." As big as the pot is, it only takes a fraction of shifter strength to move it, but Adele acts like he's cured cancer.

"Thank you so much," she cries.

Channing sits back down with a big grin on his ugly mug. I want to punch his stupid cleft chin. Why do females find him so attractive? Fuck if I know.

"Dig in," I order. Maybe if Channing starts shoveling the food in his mouth, he'll stop talking.

I grab a piece of cornbread and serve myself, but no one else makes a move. I glance up. Both of my pack members are waiting politely, looking at Adele as if she's the Alpha in charge.

"Oh, please." She waves a hand. "Don't stand on ceremony for me. Not all of us can mind our manners when we're hungry." She gives me the sweetest smile. I loosen my grip on my fork before I bend it again.

Adele hustles around the table, ladling spicy-smelling red beans over our rice. I lean back in my chair and avert my face, so I don't get a wave of her scent when she serves me. My wolf wants to grab her and lay her out on the table. I could feast for hours…

Before I lose it and grab her, Adele slips away.

Cranky, cock throbbing, I frown at my full plate. "What is this?"

"Red beans." Adele calls over her shoulder.

I fork some into my mouth. Delicious. The scent of the spices will linger here for days and drive me crazy, reminding me of her.

"I thought I told you to make us meat," I say because I'm an asshole.

"There's meat in there," Adele says. "Plenty of sausage."

"Yum," Channing says, like he's five.

Adele glows as if he's given her a compliment. "I know you said you guys like meat, but I figured I'd give you a taste of something else. Stretch your palettes a little bit."

Her smile turns mischievous. "I have several vegan entrees to try if you're willing—"

"Absolutely not." I set down my fork with a clunk. She's not the alpha here. I am. "I told you meat. Red meat. Like steak and potatoes, hold the potatoes."

"Noted," she says in a tone cold as the winter wind. "I guess you don't like red beans?"

I shrug. "It's not meat." I don't mean this as an insult, but she takes it as one. She bares her teeth like a wolf before gritting out, "This is my *mémère's* recipe." Lightning flashes from her eyes. She's so gorgeous, it takes my breath away.

"Yeah, Sarge. What's the big deal?" Channing asks around a mouth of red beans. "It's her *mémère's* recipe."

I have the insane urge to crush his skull like I did the kitchen trash can. But Adele steps close, blocking him from view.

"You want meat? That's fine." Before I know what's happening, she leans in and whisks away my plate. A few quick steps, and she's dumped it in the new kitchen trash can.

Everyone at the table goes still.

Adele marches over to the fridge, yanks the door open. She returns with a plate and slams down in front of me. "I made these just for you."

It's a pile of boiled hot dogs. At least I think they've been cooked. They're chilled from being in the fridge.

"Ketchup?" She holds up a giant bottle.

I look her right in the eye. She's not going to win this round. "Please."

She squirts ketchup all over the mountain of cold hot dogs. It looks awful, but Adele's raised eyebrow is too much of a dare. I can't back down.

I fork the top dog and start chewing like it's delicious.

The first bite sticks in my craw. I have to gulp water to get it down, but down it finally goes. A cold, hard knot that tastes like mangled pride.

Adele stands over me, her fist propped on her hip. Her green eyes are frosty. "Well?"

I raise a second awful forkful and meet her eyes. "Yum."

"Good. Glad I could accommodate you." She flounces back into the kitchen.

A coughing sound that sounds a lot like a strangled laugh comes from Deke's direction, but when I glare at him, his face is smooth, and he's focused on his plate.

"Well, I love these red beans." Channing breaks the awkward silence. "I'll eat Sarge's portion."

"Oh, there's plenty." Adele's tone is back to sugar and spice.

Channing starts to rise, plate in hand, and Adele waves him to sit.

"You don't have to stay and serve us, you know," Channing says before I can say it. I'm too busy trying to swallow another bite of hot dog.

"Oh, this is the fun part." She ladles more red beans onto his plate. "The best part of cooking is watching people enjoy it. Where I come from, food is love." And she smiles. At Channing.

And he smiles back.

The only thing keeping my wolf from leaping over the table and destroying him is years of control.

I throw down my fork. "Patrol," I snap at Channing. "Now."

Channing gives the red beans on his plate a sorrowful look, but he shoves his chair back and strides out without another word. He knows how close I am to losing it.

I'm never close to losing it. What the fuck is wrong with me?

An exasperated huff makes me turn. Adele is wrapping Channing's plate up in tin foil. Her heels strike the floor with enough force to leave sparks as she goes to the fridge to put the leftovers up, saving Channing's food for when he returns.

"Ms. Fabre, can I have a word with you in my office?"

"Absolutely," she replies immediately. Her voice is so saccharine sweet, I know she's fucking pissed at me. She whirls on her heel and sashays away in the direction of my office. Her hips sway, and my entire body tenses to keep my wolf leaping after her.

As soon as Adele disappears, I stretch leisurely, cracking my spine. My wolf thinks I'm on a hunt, and my prey is neatly cornered, in my private office.

I have got to get a grip.

Deke mops up the rest of his red beans with his last piece of cornbread. "Well, that was fun."

"Patrol for you, too," I snap.

"Yeah, I figured." He gets up unhurriedly and scrapes off his empty plate into the trash before putting it in the dishwasher. "Make sure you're in control before you go and talk to her."

"I'm always in control." My snarl echoes through the kitchen.

"Sure. Here," Deke snags the new metal trash can and hands it to me on his way out the door. "While you wait for your wolf to calm down, you can make another art sculpture."

ADELE

45

Rafe's office is a compact space with no windows, with no view to distract from total focus. Clean. Spare. Practical. Like the man himself. His desk is huge and empty except for a laptop and a pen holder with no pens. The only thing out of place is a crumpled piece of clothing in the corner. I nudge it with the toe of my shoe. It's a discarded Henley.

When I first got here, Channing gave me a mini tour and warned me that "Sarge ordered no one to bother him." Like every order Rafe gives me, I wanted to disobey right away. I was tempted to stick my head in and wave hello. Pretend to punch in. Invade his space the way he's invaded my brain.

Employee and boss. Boss and employee. That's all Rafe and I are.

I'm being a bad employee. I knew I was pushing it with the red beans and vegan comments. It's almost like I want to make him mad. Tweak his buttons. What would it be like if he lost control?

No, no, I don't want that. It's time I stop playing and fulfill my duties. Any other employer, and I'd have wowed them by now. Instead, I tested Rafe's boundaries, stirred him up, and served him cold hotdogs.

Catch more flies with honey, my mémère would say. Rafe isn't a fly, he's a big, rude, gorgeous man, with tanned skin and big, rough hands that I want to feel on my skin.

Except, no, I don't want that. I want to smack him.

"You want meat?" I mutter, pacing in front of his desk. "I'll get you meat. I'll make a turducken and shove it up your ass."

"What the hell's a turducken?" Rafe growls, and I yelp, whirling. He stands behind me, his muscle bound shoulders filling the door. For a big guy, he moves quietly.

"It's a Creole specialty," I say, trying to slow my

pounding heart. "A deboned chicken stuffed into a deboned duck. And then the duck is stuffed into a turkey." *And then I'll stuff it up your ass,* I add silently.

Rafe strides to his desk and slants me a look that tells me he heard my unspoken comment. "So I'm the turkey?"

"If the duck fits," I return sweetly.

He turns away, straightening his laptop on his desk, even though it's already straight. Is that a curve in his cheek? Is he smiling?

Does he like it when we fight as much as I do? I'm hot and bothered, my nipples hardened points beneath my pink satin and lace bra.

I realize I'm standing in front of his desk with my hands folded like I'm a student called on the carpet. I transfer my hands to my hips and try to regain my rage.

My anger is right there, waiting for me. "What the heck was that?" I snap, abandoning any pretense of sweetness. "I knew you would be rude, but this is over the top. You didn't even let them finish my food."

"You make it sound like that's a cardinal sin."

"It is."

Rafe keeps pretending to organize his desk. If he's hoping he can count to ten and we'll both calm down, he's going to be disappointed. When he looks up, I'm still glaring at him.

His beautiful face has absolutely no effect on me. None whatsoever.

His dark eyes narrow. He stalks around the desk—but I don't back up, even though my head has to tilt back, so I can keep glaring at him.

Once he's in front of his desk, he crosses his arms over his chest and leans against it. Even half sitting, he's tall enough to glower down at me. "We have a no fraternization policy in our company. The way you and Channing were flirting, I figured you both need a reminder."

What. The. Heck? "Excuse me." I hold up a finger. "I don't think that Channing's the one with the problem."

For a second, his face becomes a scarily blank mask. "Are you saying that you're the one who was flirting—"

"No," I snort. "Not him. Not me." I point my raised finger at his chest. "I'm saying it's you. You're the one with the problem, and we need to deal with it. Right now."

Rafe

Her finger hovers in the air between us. She's barely a foot away. In the small space of my dark office, her decadent scent slips around me like velvet ropes. She smells like vanilla and layers of caramel, cinnamon and a little cayenne. There's not much light in my office—I chose a secure space with no windows—but the harsh glow from the desk lamp is enough to illuminate her perfect face. Her brown skin glows, lustrous as a pearl. Her eyes are a stunning blend of brown and green in dark rims.

"Did you hear me, Mr. Lightfoot?" She uses my last name because I used hers. I'm trying to put some distance between us, but it's not working. The more I retreat, the more I ache to clutch her close. To touch that sweet feminine body of hers and make her breath catch in her throat. Choke on my name.

"Rafe," I mutter. "Call me Rafe."

"Rafe, then," she says in a softer tone, and my head jerks up like I got a bullet to the chest. For once, she follows orders, and my name on her lips almost knocks me down. "Like I was saying, we've got some unresolved business. We better resolve it if this is going to work."

Business. Work. Is that all this is to her?

I can't do it. I can't be her boss. I can't stay away.

With one step, I close the space between us.

ADELE

Rafe's heat slams into me the moment before his arm cages me. He hauls me close against his hard body. I'm torn between wanting to slap him and wanting to swoon like Scarlett in Rhett's arms.

"See, this is exactly the problem," I say, even though my heart is thumping a mile a minute.

Red crests his cheeks. "Stop talking," he mutters.

"Excuse me?" How dare he try to silence me. I open my mouth, but his eyes flare with an odd green light, and I gulp my insult down. From a distance, Rafe is beautiful. Up close, he stuns me to silence. Green light flashes when he dips his head close. There's a mini Aurora Borealis, dancing in his eyes. "What's that?" I touch his jaw without thinking. "What's going on with your eyes?"

"For fuck's sake, stop talking." Rough fingers slip into my curls, and Rafe tugs back my head. The move bares my face and my throat to him.

One moment, his hard features fill my vision. Angry black brows, wild eyes. The next, his soft lips are on mine.

Our first kiss is violent. An argument, a fight. Bruising, taking no prisoners. It's wonderful.

He advances, and I retreat without thinking, only stopping when my back hits a wall. His leg wedges between mine, forcing me to straddle the hard ridge of his thigh. His body is a taut prison around me, huge and masculine.

I flatten my palms against his shoulders. I meant to push him away, but instead, my hands find the granite-like biceps, and I clutch him closer. Another tug on my hair, and he breaks the kiss.

I pant, every cell in my body electrified, heat tingling everywhere he's touched me.

"No," he says, the sharp planes of his face turned away from mine. "We can't do this."

"Fuck you," I snap back. "Stop thinking and kiss me."

A growl rumbles in his chest, but he obeys, his perfect lips sipping, tugging, demanding more. I drink of him, lost and drunk on his whiskey taste.

My hips surge, rocking upwards. Searching for and finding the iron edge of his thick thigh. Now I'm riding his thigh with my cute vintage 1950s swing dress crushed between us. The crisp skirts and crinoline slide up my thighs. One of my Mary Jane pumps falls off with a clunk. I don't even care.

I'm a mess, in total disarray. He destroyed all my control and poise in five fucking seconds.

And I love it.

"Rafe," I murmur. He kisses down my neck, the scrape of his stubble chafing my soft skin. The delicious prickle zings from my throat to my nipples and detonates in my core.

"No." Rafe jerks his head back and leans away. Without him to prop me up, I slide down the wall.

"Oh my God," I breathe. In the absence of his heated body, a chill washes over me. I just made out with Rafe. In his office.

"Fuck," he explodes and turns away.

Yes! Fuck me! I barely catch myself from begging. My lips are puffy, bruised in the most delicious way. I touch them, wanting to savor the memory of Rafe's mouth on mine.

I just made out with my boss. I stop caressing and scrub my lips instead.

There's a tense moment while I straighten my skirts and find my missing shoe. I check with shaking hands to make sure all my buttons are buttoned. My core is throbbing, and I'm sure my panties have melted off.

Rafe's back is to me, his hands planted on the desk. His entire body is rigid, his shoulders bunched around his ears.

Kissing was a mistake, but we both made it. I refuse to apologize. I shake my disheveled curls out of my face and clear my throat. "This meeting could've been an email."

"Yeah."

"Good." I nod even though he can't see me. "See you tomorrow." And I flounce out as fast as my pumps can carry me.

Rafe

I stand in my office for a long time after Adele leaves, breathing in her scent. My wolf is confused. Why didn't I take her? Mark her?

To the wolf, the world is simple. If you're hungry, hunt prey and eat. If you find your mate, claim her.

I can't, I tell it. *I can't have a mate.*

My phone rings, and I answer it without checking who it is.

It's Colonel Johnson, but his gruff voice does little to stir me out of my haze. "There's movement with Dieter. He's left Italy."

I sit behind my desk and pick up a pen as if it'll help me focus. There are still drops of ink from its exploded predecessor. "Dieter," just saying my nemesis' name is

51

enough to call my thoughts back. What does he know about me? About my parents' death? "Where is he?"

"We tracked him to Paris but lost him there. We're monitoring the situation. There's no word of any deals, so he's probably headed to another hideyhole."

"Any new intel on how he knew to use silver bullets?"

"No."

"Colonel, I–"

"Your orders are to stand down," Johnson barks. His tone softens. "I know you want to go after him, son. I'm asking you to follow orders until we know more."

"Yes sir." There's a pop and a splash of liquid over my hand, but I don't look down. I broke another pen.

"Keep your pack close," he orders and hangs up.

My pack. Right. They're the most important thing in the world to me. Deke and Channing are on patrol. Lance is in town, safe with his mate. I need to focus on them.

My parents, lying cold and still on the cabin floor. Blood pooled under their heads...

No! It won't happen again. I will keep control, keep my pack safe.

I have no time for Adele. She doesn't fit into my life, and that's the way things are. That's the way things gotta be.

5

Rafe

"Dinner is served." It's shift two of Adele's job, and she's back at the lodge, waving all of us to the table. This time Sadie joined us. I invited her so we'd be on our best behavior.

"Adele, this looks great," Sadie gushes. And it does. Huge silver domes cover our plates. We lift them together. I brace myself, expecting hotdogs. But no, it's steak. About six of them, stacked high on my plate. Giant, thick cuts of meat.

My wolf is officially in love.

"Aww, yeah," Deke mutters. Next to him, his mate Sadie shoots him a grin.

"Meat. As ordered," Adele announces. "All different cuts. There's ribeye, tenderloin and Porterhouse. And filet mignon for the ladies."

"Thanks for that." Sadie's voice holds laughter. Her plate has a much smaller cut of meat and what looks like some roasted asparagus on the side.

"Oh, I love filet mignon," Channing says around a mouthful of meat.

"There are a few little ones left over. You can have them for breakfast," Adele says. She's leaning against the kitchen island, watching us eat.

I hook the chair next to me with my foot and pull it out. "Sit," I order.

She lifts a slim brown brow. I arch one of mine in return. A little smile flits over her face and away. There's a little pink in her cheeks, and my cock stirs. We're both thinking of our last, brief meeting in the office.

A few more seconds—she always hesitates before obeying, and I love it—and she clops over in her high heels. As soon as she's seated, I cut my ribeye in half and serve her some steak.

The guys side-eye me. When an alpha gives up some of his meat, his kill, to someone, it's a big deal. It means that they're special in his life.

And of course, Adele's special. She's my chef. My employee. Friend of my pack brother's mate.

My wolf rumbles in my chest, disagreeing. We both know she means more than that. He thinks I'm an idiot.

I think I'm an idiot too. Why in the hell am I subjecting myself to this torture?

Then Adele's arm brushes mine, and she leans close. "Your stomach is rumbling, Rafe," she murmurs, and fuck if I don't get hard at the mere sound of my name on her tongue.

ADELE

"Do you have indigestion already?" I tease gently. I've

promised myself I'd behave around Rafe from now on. But I can't help poking him a little. "Your stomach sounds like an angry bear."

"More like a wolf," Channing mumbles around a mouthful of food. I didn't realize he could hear my lowered voice.

Rafe frowns in Channing's direction, and I lean a bit closer. I don't know why Rafe gets so edgy when I pay attention to Channing, but I promised myself tonight would be a truce. "Well?" I ask Rafe, ignoring Channing. "Is the poison I put in your portion kicking in?"

Rafe snorts. "Nah. Just need more meat in me." He saws off a huge portion of ribeye, but instead of ripping into it, he slaps it onto my plate.

"You need to eat," he grunts. Once again ordering me around.

"*You* need to eat," I return sweetly. "You didn't eat much at dinner yesterday. You'll start losing muscle mass unless you finish all your meat." I tap his biceps. His hard, outrageously swole bicep. If he lost some muscle mass, he'd still be buffer than most of the fitness models in a *Men's Health* magazine.

He slants me a look, and I realize I'm still resting my palm on his arm. "You done?"

I pretend it's on purpose and give it a little squeeze. Hot damn, his muscle is huge. Hard and honed by his work as a badass, protecting people from bad guys. I allow myself one more squeeze, and then I drop my hand.

The look Rafe is giving me is hot enough to set me on fire.

I clear my throat and focus on my now full plate. "How's the steak? Is it too rare?"

"No such thing," Rafe says.

"Good. Save room for dessert," I chide.

"There's dessert?" Channing looks so adorably eager. I let myself laugh at his expression, even though I know it annoys Rafe. I like annoying Rafe. It's like foreplay—not that we're going to go any further.

"Yes," I say. "A red velvet cake with cream cheese frosting. I decorated it to look like a Jersey cow." I wrinkle my nose at Rafe. "You can pretend you're eating ribeye the entire time."

He holds my gaze as he takes his next bite.

My cheeks warm and everyone at the table watches us. Channing and Deke are stuffing their faces with steak, but Sadie has a satisfied look on her face. Hmmm.

Boss and employee. Employee and boss. That's all Rafe and I are to each other.

"Nice weather we're having," I say to fill the silence.

Deke cranes his neck. "If you like snow," he says.

"Guess I'm staying the night," Sadie murmurs. She and Deke share a look that shouts *Let's fuck like bunnies!* so loud I blush harder and look away to give them privacy.

"That reminds me, Adele," Rafe's low voice carries over the entire table. Everyone falls silent as if they're waiting for him to make an important pronouncement. Maybe that's why Rafe acts like he's in charge all the time. Everyone treats him like he's the boss. "I don't want you driving home by yourself."

The bottom half of my jaw falls to the floor. "Excuse me?"

He keeps eating like what he said is perfectly reasonable. "The weather isn't good. You need new tires."

Oh no, he didn't just call attention to my old truck. Is this some sort of dig on how broke I am right now? "My tires will be fine for tonight," I say calmly.

He shakes his head. "I'll drive you home and pick you

up around lunch tomorrow. We'll keep your truck here and put on the new tires."

"I don't think that's in our contract," I say.

He shrugs and pats his mouth with his napkin. "Consider it an addendum."

"Maybe we should discuss this in your office," I say. Everyone's eyes ping back and forth between Rafe and me like we're playing a tennis match. Which we are. Not tennis, but a verbal fight. *To the death.*

"No need to discuss it. I'm driving you home. That's final."

I blink at my plate. If I look at Rafe, steam is going to boil out of my head.

Sadie's eyes are wide. "So, about dessert…"

"Yeah, dessert sounds good," Deke mutters. His plate is already empty. So is Channing's. Rafe wasn't kidding when he said they could pack it away.

"I'll get it," I leap up. "Y'all keep eating." I practically sprint into the kitchen. I need a break from Rafe.

But the big bastard follows me. "I mean it, princess," he says in a low voice.

"Princess?" I raise a brow, ignoring the little thrill at the nickname. I am not flattered that Rafe gave me a nickname. I refuse to be.

He catches my elbow as I pass and growls in my ear. "You're not driving in this."

Visions of turduckens dance in my head. Rafe's lucky I don't have a deboning knife handy.

"Your food is getting cold," I reply.

"I mean it," he murmurs, still holding me.

"Do you grab all your employees like this?" I ask.

He lets me go. I swipe the cake off the marble-topped island and march back to the dining table. "Dessert," I announce. I look right at Rafe as I hold up the giant carving knife and plunge it into the cake.

His face holds no expression as I carve dessert up and serve it. The red velvet interior looks shocking, just like I planned.

"You know, Sarge is right," Channing says. "I think we have tires that will work on your truck—we order good ones for our vehicles, and it's cheaper to buy in bulk. It'd be no trouble to fix you up."

"Well, thank you then." I force a little smile to my lips. The act of charity still rankles, but Channing understands how to talk to a person. Rafe and I need to take lessons from him.

You catch more flies with honey. But if I give Rafe a taste of my honey, he'd enjoy it too much. *He'd lick it all up...*

Crap, now I'm thinking of Rafe licking things. Things that belong to me.

Everyone has their head down, eating. Everyone but Rafe. He's still staring at me with his hard gaze. We're back in our tennis match, and the score is love-love.

"You're not eating your cake," I say.

"That's because it looks like someone murdered it."

"That was the intent." And because that's not homicidal enough, I swipe a finger up the knife and lick frosting off my finger. "You know, Channing, maybe you can drive me home. I'm sure Rafe is terribly busy." Busy being an asshole.

"Yeah, sure," Channing says around a mouthful of cake.

Rafe shoves back his chair and throws down his fork. "Channing, I need to see you outside. Now."

What the heck? Who the fuck does Rafe think he is, ordering Channing around like a disobedient toddler?

But Channing obeys. Both he and Rafe stomp out of the dining room.

To my surprise, Deke follows. "Thanks for the food," he mutters as he passes me.

Sadie sighs and pushes out of her own chair.

"Wait, what's happening?" I say. Five seconds ago, this table was full, and now everybody's leaving. They really do follow Rafe's orders.

"They're going to fight," Sadie says she doesn't sound shocked at all.

"What about dessert?"

"Oh, they'll be back," Sadie calls over her shoulder. "They'll be hungry after the fight."

Again the lower half of my jaw sways in the breeze. I set down the knife and hurry after Sadie.

Rafe

I'm going to kill this fucking motherfucker. Channing lopes out the door and into the cold night, his muscles straining under his shirt. His wolf is frantic to burst out, defend itself.

"You don't talk to Adele." My growl is half human, half wolf, one hundred percent savage. "You don't look at her. You don't see her. You don't smell her."

"You're crazy, Sarge," Channing grunts, stripping off his Henley and tossing it on the stone steps. He doesn't look worried. He wants a fight as badly as I do.

"No animals," I order. We can't risk showing Adele our wolves. If she finds out what I am, she'll run from me to never return.

And I can't have that. Even though I can't have her.

"Just claim her already," Channing's eyes glint with a

wild blue light. His wolf looking out from his face. "You want to. You know what she is to you."

No.

It can't be.

Adele is a civilian. She's nothing more than an employee. An acquaintance. She barely tolerates me. "You know I can't do that. I can't claim a human." Even though Deke did. Even though my brother Lance did.

A mate, a family, that's not for me.

"If you won't claim her, you're going to go moon mad," Channing warns. He's speaking the truth, and I hate it.

"Not gonna happen. I'm not going to claim her."

We start to circle each other, our boots crunching on the frosty grass.

Channing gives a wild grin. He looks as crazy as I feel, and I know what he's going to say before he says it. "If you won't claim her, then maybe I will."

I snarl and launch my fist at his face.

ADELE

The front lawn of the lodge has a fresh coat of white. Sadie's already out there on the stoop, her body blocking most of my view through the glass panes of the front door. I pull on my coat and hat. It looks freezing out there, and more snow's drifting down. Are Channing and Rafe really going to fight? In this weather?

What the heck is wrong with these guys? Talk about macho men. Is this an overdose of testosterone? I should not be feeding them meat. I should be feeding them... I don't know... soybeans or yams or something, for the estrogen. They need to take a freaking chill pill.

Bracing myself for the blast of cold air, I dash out of the door. My boots do skid a little bit on the icy stoop. Damn it, Rafe was right about wearing heeled boots in the snow. But for goodness sake, how often do I need to run in boots?

I push the door closed behind me, already shivering. Sadie stands on the stone steps, her body swathed in her big down coat and her shoulders hunched a little. Down on the path, Deke's standing with his hands in his pockets. He looks almost bored. We're all breathing smoke into the cold air, and Deke's not even wearing a coat!

Fat snowflakes float lazily to earth, spots of white in the dark night. I shade my eyes against the harsh overhead flood lights to peer into the dark lawn. The lodge is set into the side of the mountain, surrounded by thick evergreen forest. Rafe and Channing are out there, two dark shapes blending with the pines.

My eyes adjust, and I catch my breath. Rafe and Channing are half naked. No winter coats, no hats. No shirts at all. They've both ripped off their Henleys and are circling each other, their boots tamping down the fluffy snow. Their torsos flex as they move. They look like participants in some insane bodybuilding martial art competition. For some reason, it just now occurs to me that the fight might be over *me*. With quick, fluid movements, they bob and weave, and then in a blur they throw themselves at each other.

A cry leaps from my mouth before I can stop it. My hand flies up to my face as if I can catch the sound. The fighters grapple now, rough grunts and guttural growls escaping.

"This is crazy," I whisper. Because, seriously, what the heck? Why are these guys fighting? Did I miss the memo? It's it WWE night?

Sadie's hooded head turns, and she gives me a sympathetic smile. "It's a little intense. But this is how they get out their energy." She doesn't sound worried at all. "Don't worry, no one gets hurt."

Deke glances back at us and moves down the path, his big body in direct line between us and the fighters. I get the feeling if the fight came our way, Deke would prevent us from getting hurt.

But he's not doing anything to stop the vicious pounding Rafe and Channing are giving each other.

Rafe's right arm flies back, and he throws a punch that Channing blocks somehow. With a blurred movement, Rafe punches with his left fist. The surprise attack breaks through. Channing's head snaps back, and he staggers. Any normal man would be down on the grass after a hit like that, but Channing bounces right back looking almost cheerful as he spits blood. His dimple flashes, and he rushes Rafe, hitting him in the torso and making them both land hard on the ground. Now they're thrashing around on the ground. Shirtless. In the snow.

"Stop," I holler, scrambling down the stone steps to the lawn. "What are you doing?"

"Stay back," Deke orders, holding out a big, cold chapped hand.

"Adele, it's okay," Sadie says quickly, coming to stand beside me. Seriously? She's a kindergarten teacher. Doesn't she believe in better forms of conflict resolution?

"No, it's not," I mutter. I knew these guys were adrenaline and testosterone junkies, but this is over the top.

What's worse, a flush is working its way up my chest. The sight of Rafe, his epic muscles on display, is making me feel some kind of way. Inside my blouse, my breasts swell.

Who knew watching Rafe fight would be such a turn

on? I clench my right hand into a fist to keep from fanning my face.

I need to stop this fight.

In her day, my mémère had to break up a few fights from the rough and tumble men staying at her boarding house. I frantically try to remember those stories now. One time Mémère had a pot of hot coffee, and she threw it in one of the fighter's faces. The contents of the pot weren't too hot, and according to Mémère, everyone ended up laughing it off.

Maybe that story was a wee bit embellished over the years. Right now, in the tense thick of the moment, I don't see how it could be true.

I don't have any hot coffee. I don't have anything. I would tip a whole pot of gumbo over them if it would make them stop.

Channing's on his back in the snowy grass. Next thing I see is Rafe's body fly back toward the trees. "Ha!" Channing shouts, and with a snap of both legs, he launches himself up and back onto his feet.

Rafe rushes him. In a movement too fast for me to see, Rafe somehow gets Channing in a hold and flips him. Now Channing is the one flying across the lawn.

I'm wringing my hands. "This is nuts," I snap. I dash back inside the house to see if there's anything I can grab to throw at them. The first thing my eyes light on is the crumpled metal sculpture Rafe made. Someone moved it to a coffee table. I snatch it up and rush back out.

The fight has come closer to the door. Deke has both hands out, blocking Sadie with his whole body. He's so intent on protecting her, I'm able to slip past him.

"Stop," I scream and hurl the metal sculpture at Rafe. It falls short, clunking onto the path and rolling a little.

Rafe and Channing pause in the midst of trying to punch each other's lights out to stare at it.

"Will you freaking stop?" I charge forward, careful not to get too close.

"Adele, no," Sadie cries. Before I take another step, Deke catches me around the waist. My feet move, but I'm walking on air.

"Put me down," I huff.

"Promise you won't try to break up the fight." Still holding me, Deke gives me a shake.

Channing and Rafe are already circling each other again, the distraction forgotten.

They don't want me to get involved? Fine. I won't get involved.

"Whatever," I mutter, and Deke pivots, setting me behind him on the path. He keeps a big hand gripping my arm, over the sleeve of my puffy down jacket. "Let me go." I start to shake him off.

Out on the lawn, Rafe's head snaps in our direction. His face contorts. His eyes blaze with a green light.

"Shit," Deke mutters. He lets me go and holds his hands up in the air like Rafe just pointed a gun. "It's all right, Sarge. She's all right. No one's touching her."

Rafe bares his teeth like he's a feral dog...and growls. My spine tingles at the sound.

"Was just trying to make sure she was safe," Deke mutters in a low, rough voice, his hands still outstretched, but Rafe doesn't seem to hear him.

"Shit," Channing's eyes go wide, and he races across the lawn. "Sarge—"

Channing's too late. Before Channing can grab him, Rafe launches himself at Deke.

Sadie and I both cry out. She grabs me and tugs me

back to the steps. Clutching each other's coats, we steady each other and scramble back to the door.

Wild snarls fill the night air. Rafe is whaling on Deke, who's defending himself and punching back. Channing wades into the fight, trying to pull Rafe off Deke. With a roar, Rafe shakes Channing off and chases after Deke.

"That's it." I announce to the frosty air. "I'm out of here." It's a wonder my voice isn't shaking.

"Adele…" Sadie starts and bites her lip.

"No, no." I raise a hand. "This is ridiculous. Y'all have too much testosterone going on here." I get my coat and my keys. In the past few minutes, the snowfall has lessened.

My little truck sits bravely in the driveway, and as I approach her, I study my tires with new eyes. They aren't bald, but they're closer to bald than new. I need to put car maintenance higher on my list of things to do. But Rafe is not going to take me home and fix my tires. No way.

The fight has moved across the lawn, closer to the black line of trees. Good. Let them kill each other, I don't care.

I march down the path to the driveway, muttering to myself, "He told me not to drive my truck? He wants me to let him drive me home? Too freaking bad." He shouldn't have acted like a drunken maniac and picked a fight.

I can't work under these conditions. At this point, I'd be happy never to see Rafe again.

Rafe

"For fuck's sake, Sarge," Deke takes a punch to the gut and grunts. He's a big fucker, and he's used to taking hits. He's the crazy one—he used to pick fights all the time. It annoyed the shit outta me.

Now I'm the one who wants to rip the world apart.

"Don't fucking touch her," I punctuate each word with my fist. Deke blocks half the blows, retreating into the woods. I've noticed he's been drawing me away from the house and his mate.

Sadie's on the stoop by the front door, pressing her lips together. Adele is...gone. My wolf is frantic, trying to tell me something. The rage is receding.

Before I can ask where Adele is, Channing slams into me. His arms go around me.

"He's not touching her," Channing bawls. "He was making sure she's safe."

"I fucking know!" I grunt. "Get the fuck off!"

"Quick," Channing yells to Deke. "Sit on him!"

Deke wades in. I thrash, breaking Channing's grip and scrambling to my feet. Deke's coming at me. I feint left, then right, and punch him in the gut, hard enough to break a rib. Channing grabs me from behind, and I slam my head back into his face. Blood sprays.

"Fugh." Channing's down on his back in the snow, holding his nose.

"Fuck," Deke grunts, gritting his teeth and pressing a hand to his side.

With no one around me, I look around wildly for Adele. Her scent is fading in the night air. I pay attention to what the wolf is telling me—and I hear it. The sound of her old truck's engine, heading down the drive.

She left. She's gone.

"Fuck," I shout. She's upset, and she's driving her beater through the snow. I gotta go after her.

"I got it, Sarge." Deke's already stripped out of his boots and shirt. He shucks off his fatigues and a huge black wolf tears out of his body. A second later, it's bounding away, it's big paws allowing more purchase on the snow-covered ground.

"I'm right behind you," I call as Deke disappears into the dark woods. He'll follow her down the drive and buy me a few minutes to follow.

I take stock of myself. No broken bones. A twinge in my elbow—but it's already healing. I turn to Channing, but he's already reset his broken nose. Neither of us are breathing hard.

My wolf's eager to get after Adele, but I need to check on my packmate first. Fuck, I completely lost it.

I'll think about it later.

Channing sits up. His eye sockets are shadowed with the remains of two black eyes. He spits more blood and grins. "All good, Sarge?" he asks as if I wasn't just pummeling his face with both fists.

"All good." I offer him a hand up and pull him close for a manly hug, complete with back slaps. This is how a pack fights and makes up. Unless it's an alpha fight, a fight for dominance, a fight to the death, we scrap together and forget it all within moments.

Sadie's already come to collect Deke's boots and clothes. She hands Channing his Henley helpfully. She's a gem of a woman, perfect for a shifter mate. Although her brow is knotted.

"I didn't see your shirt," she says.

"I'm good. We're all good," I reassure her.

She nods and glances down the road. "These roads are really icy," she whispers to me, and I nod. She's worried about Adele.

So am I.

"Go back in the house," I tell Sadie. "It'll be okay. Deke and I will make sure she's safe."

I turn to Channing, and he nods before I can say

67

anything. "I'll watch the lodge. Go on, Sarge. Go get your female."

Your female. I don't waste time correcting him. I turn and run with shifter speed through the woods, following Deke's wolf tracks.

~

ADELE

My fingers clutch the cold steering wheel, my body tense as if I can will my vehicle safely down the snowy drive. I should've waited longer for my truck to warm up. My breath is fog in front of my face. The snow's picked up again, and my old tires aren't handling the road well.

Who the hell lives on the side of a mountain with only a hellish, winding road to reach them? Rafe Lightfoot is officially the most annoying man on earth.

I still can't get over the fierce snarl on his face. He looked like a madman. Wild. Feral. He looked like something not human.

I hope poor Channing's all right. He got a few punches in, but he acted like it was all a game. Rafe wasn't acting. He looked like he wanted to murder someone, and Channing happened to be game.

Deke and Sadie didn't seem to care. Maybe it turned out all right. Maybe I should've stayed and heard the explanation. Maybe after they got their tensions out, they all went back inside and had coffee and dessert.

The real reason I left: Rafe's gorgeous body, half naked, muscles flexing. Flawless. Scrumptious. The things I would do to that man if I got him alone.

My tires skid a little, and only years of practice stops me from hitting the brake and sliding into a ditch.

Stop thinking about him. I need to focus, not think about

getting Rafe alone after the fight, his hard body sleek with sweat, his heated gaze locked onto my body.

Focus. My windshield is fogging up, and the defroster vents are doing nothing to help. I lean forward and wipe the glass clean with my coat sleeve. It clears the glass a little, but leaves a smear. *Goddammit.*

A few more yards, and the narrow drive deposits me onto a bigger road, and I breathe a little easier. Maybe I will get down the mountain after all.

Something flashes at me in the dark. Two green lights, glowing. Some sort of animal loping out of the forest. A dark shape, with light tipped ears—a wolf. It sits and watches my truck inch down the snowy road, looking regal and calm. Unafraid. I shouldn't take my eyes off the road, but I do, just for a second, to stare at it.

And that's when my tires hit black ice.

Rafe

I hear the accident before I see it. A crunch of metal and then silence. I tear down the mountain, a bit slower than shifter speed, so I don't lose my step and go tumbling. It'd be easier to do this as a wolf. My body would be closer to the ground.

The road is a white ribbon through the dark trees. I speed my steps. There's Deke up ahead. He's a huge beast, black with white tipped ears. I'm dashing now, not bothering to be careful. Branches whip my face. One catches my mouth, and I taste blood.

Deke the wolf turns and trots up the incline to meet me, and I feel relief. He wouldn't be so calm if Adele was hurt. He'd be down there, shifted to a naked human to help her.

"She alive?" I ask. The wolf nods.

"Go. Get Channing and the Hummer." We have good snow tires on the Humvee.

Another dip of its big, furry head and the wolf runs off.

I continue down, just slow enough to keep from over-balancing, letting gravity pull me down. Adele's truck is half off the road, canted into a ditch. The driver's side of tires spin in the air.

I sniff the air as I slide down the final few yards of the embankment. There's no scent of blood, but she could be hurt internally.

ADELE

I took my eyes off the road for a second, and now I'm in a ditch. My tires slid out from under me.

The thump and crunch echo in my ears. My cab is tilted, but I'm still in my seat thanks to my seatbelt.

I'm alive. The world has gone silent, and the snow seems to be falling in slow motion.

The wolf is gone. Apparently car accidents disturb it because as soon as I looked up, it was loping back up the hill and disappeared into the forest.

My truck's not quite on its side, but it's off the road. Stuck in a ditch. Not driveable. My purse has slid to the far right. Looks like it spilled its contents out onto the floor. I would have to shift my weight in my seat to get my seat belt unbuckled, then crawl over the seats to get my phone. Not that my phone will do any good. I never get cell service here.

The cold is already seeping into my cab—hell, it never left. The snow is already accumulating on my windshield.

What the heck am I going to do?

At least it's quiet here. Peaceful. I'll have a beautiful view as I freeze to death.

"Adele." Someone barks and rips my truck door open.

It's Rafe. He's still shirtless, and he looks like something out of my fantasies. Hair wild, jaw clenched, every muscle taut with movement. His eyes flash green. For a moment his eyes look a lot like that wolf's.

"Hang on," he growls. "I've got you."

I tamp down the insane joy I feel at seeing him.

"I'm okay," I say. My voice is so calm. "No need to——"

There's a tear as he rips my seat belt *with his bare hands*. I didn't know seatbelts could tear like that. Mine must be dry rotted or something. *I really need to do more maintenance on this car.*

And then I'm in Rafe's arms. His muscles bunch and flex right before my eyes.

"It's okay, baby," he murmurs.

Baby.

I wouldn't have thought of him as the endearment type. We certainly weren't at that point, despite our mutual attraction, but hearing it makes something in me turn soft and gooey. Pivoting as if my weight is nothing, he climbs out of the ditch. Just like that, he's standing on the road, me in his arms. He makes no move to put me down.

I give into the urge and snuggle close. He's so warm. Even without a coat. How does he stand the cold without a coat?

He lets me snuggle. He must understand I'd never do this normally, but right now there are extenuating circumstances

"Are you hurt?" he asks. "Did you hit your head?"

"No." It's true. I'm not hurt at all. The accident was stupid, but I'm incredibly lucky.

My ride is not so lucky. My poor truck looks so sad, wedged in the snow.

"Hang on," Rafe says. He's already striding up the road. "I'll get you home."

"What about my truck?" My teeth are chattering but not only from the cold. There's sweat running down my back. My adrenaline is surging.

"Deke and Channing will take care of it," he mutters.

"How do they know I had an accident?" Not that I'm complaining. I would've sat shivering for hours, hoping someone would happen to drive past and see me.

He pauses. "I had a feeling."

"A feeling? So you drove after me?" No, wait, there's no sign of his car. "You ran? All this way?"

"Had to make sure you were safe," he mutters, almost too low for me to hear.

I bite my lip to hide the happiness that spreads through me. He hasn't said, *I told you so* yet. For that, I'm grateful. He's marching, no, jogging back up the road where we came.

"You can say it," I tell him. "You can say *I told you so.*"

"It's my fault you got in the accident."

What? "No it's not. I'm the one who drove off the road."

"It's my fault you left."

"That's not... No." He can't possibly think that, it's ridiculous. I stare at his beautiful face. His eyes are fixed on the road, his dark brows knotted, the blade of his jaw iron hard. A piece of the Rafe puzzle falls into place. He's the Sarge, the leader of his posse. Yeah, he orders everyone around, and it's annoying, but it's because he takes everyone's well-being as his responsibility. He'd probably do anything to protect his team. He'll lead the way, but he'll also eat last.

I know exactly what he's like because I'm the same way.

"Rafe, you're not responsible for me."

He doesn't say anything, but I can sense him fighting not to argue.

I can't stop my grin. I'm giddy with this new knowledge about Rafe. "I can hear you disagreeing."

"It's my job to keep you safe," he says in that way of his. That *I know what's best, and that's final* manner I found so annoying. Now it's warming me from the inside out.

"I'm an adult, I can make my own decisions. I can leave on my own. And when I get into an accident, I can own it."

"Fine," he says.

"Fine," I repeat, pretending to be snippy. "So it is my fault."

"Sure, baby. It's your fault."

"As long as we're clear."

The corner of his mouth twitches, and I touch it, push it up into a real half smile.

We're arguing, but we're smiling. Is arguing our thing? Oh my God, is this how we flirt?

He gives me a searing look, and I drop my hand before I do something ridiculous. Like kiss him.

Is the night still cold? I'm burning up.

Rafe turns off the road and starts hiking up the side of the hillside.

"What are you doing?" I ask as he plunges us into the woods.

"This way is faster," he mutters.

"Maybe if you're some sort of macho extreme mountain man." Oops, I said that out loud.

"Macho extreme mountain man?" he repeats and grins. A real grin, not a shadow of one.

73

"You heard me." I lock my arms around his neck and lay my head back on his shoulder. "Thank you for coming for me," I add quietly.

He hitches me closer. His jaw brushes the top of my head as he murmurs, "I'll always come for you."

6

Adele

Back at the lodge, there's a black square in the driveway where Rafe's Humvee is usually parked. "Deke and Channing took your car?" I don't pretend I haven't noticed the badass vehicle Rafe drives.

"It's got good tires," Rafe says. "Handles great in the snow." His lips press together like he's trying to keep them from curling up into a smile.

"'That was almost an *I told you so*. You must be feeling more yourself." His jaw is still clenched, but he's not even breathing hard.

I loosen my grip on Rafe's shoulders as he starts up the path. It's been fun being carried, but it's over.

"Guess we missed the guys, hiking through the woods like that," I chatter. "How did they know to drive down to get my truck?"

"I told them to do it."

I squint at him. "Because you had a feeling."

"Yes."

Hmmm. Something isn't adding up, but I'm too distracted to think it through. Maybe I did hit my head.

Sadie opens the door right as Rafe walks up to it.

"Oh my God, Adele," she gasps. "Are you okay?"

"It's all right," I say, waving to her. "I'm fine. I slid off the road, but I think it'll be fine."

Her brow is still furrowed, but she lets out a sigh of relief. Rafe strides into the house, right past her. He doesn't look left or right.

"Rafe, put me down."

"No."

I start to struggle. "What will Sadie think?" She's still standing by the door. Now she looks like she's about to laugh.

"We're adults, remember? We can make our own decisions." He keeps carrying me through the house.

"I don't think this is a good idea." Me. Rafe. Alone.

"It's an excellent idea."

"Just put me down." I start to squirm but get nowhere. God gave Rafe extra muscles and almost none to me. "Rafe—"

"Stop talking," he mutters.

So annoying! If it were any other man I'd slap him. But...I want to see what he does next. I shut my mouth and let him carry me up the stairs, down the long hall to the bedroom at the end. Looks like I'm going to get to see Rafe's bedroom after all.

It's massive. There's a fireplace on one wall. A huge four poster bed with a leather headboard dominates the space. There's a leather chair on the side, angled so it can take in the view of the mountains. The back wall is mostly windows. There are no curtains, just an amazing unadulterated view of the mountain range covered with snow-covered pines. The outside feels close enough I could reach out and touch it.

"Rafe, you're getting slush everywhere," I fuss. I don't want him to ruin this beautiful wood floor or the thick rug. He has a great taste in decor, I have to give him that. The space is striking and masculine yet comfortable at the same time.

He sets me down in front of the fireplace, but his big hands keep hold of my coat. "I need to see if you're hurt." He unzips me and tugs my coat off before I know what's happening.

"I'm okay, Rafe. It was stupid, and you were ..." The word sticks in my throat. "You were right about the tires. About the snow." I grab his wrist.

"Let me do it, princess," he says. "Let me make sure you're not hurt." He lifts the hem of my silk shirt, peeling it up over my breasts.

"Oh," I choke in surprise. I lift my arms to allow him to pull it over my head. I'm wearing a pale pink silk and lace bra that makes my brown skin glow. The demi cup offers up my breasts while leaving most of my skin bare.

An animal-like rumble leaves his throat as his green gaze drinks it in. "That's pretty." He works the zipper on my pencil skirt. "So damn pretty." His voice sounds thick and guttural. There's no mistaking the hunger in his movements, in his gaze.

"Wh-what are we doing?" I meant to say *what are you doing*, but I admit I'm a part of this. I'm the one letting him undress me in front of his fireplace. My pussy clenches as thrills of excitement run through me.

"We're debriefing."

"Debriefing?" Sounds official, very military, but I have no idea what that means.

"Mmm hmm. First I'm going to check you for

injuries," he rumbles. "Then I'm going to punish you for putting yourself in danger."

"Excuse me?" Unfortunately, my words come out quavery and excited rather than assertive.

He slides down my skirt, unwrapping me like a present. My clothing falls to the floor, and Rafe goes still as a hunter sighting a deer, taking me in.

I lick my lips. I didn't think Rafe would ever see my garter belt and stockings, but that didn't stop me from fantasizing something like this moment when I put them on this morning.

"Fate help me," he murmurs as he strokes his warm palms up my thighs. It's an odd turn of phrase, but Rafe is a singular man. "Did you wear this for me?" His hand skims up my leg.

"No," I shoot back, albeit a little breathlessly. "I wear lingerie like this all the time." It's true. My mémère believed a woman would be more confident if she wore silk and satin and lace and nice things against her skin. A secret luxury for her and only her–and maybe a partner if she so chose. And so a portion of my paycheck has always gone to making sure I have beautiful bras and camisoles and panties and, yes, even garter belts.

"You mean to tell me you wear stuff like this under your clothes all this time?" Rafe looks almost angry. Or is he frustrated?

"Of course," I give a little shrug and lean back a little to show off my body. The garter belt's straps skim down my legs to clip to silk stockings. The ensemble frames my pussy perfectly.

Rafe growls a little as he explores me. His touch is even lighter than I imagined it would be, his hands rough but so gentle.

I bite my lip. I lied. I don't always wear garter belts.

When I put it on this morning, I imagined Rafe holding my waist just as he is now.

He kneels in front of me, his face right where I need him, so I find any protests I might have produced melt away like snowflakes on warm skin. He presses a kiss against the front of my panties, right at the apex of my slit.

I catch the back of his head and hold him there. He opens his mouth, and I squirm against the sensation of his hot breath through the thin fabric. He nips my nether lips through the panties, and I moan.

"You disobeyed me, princess." His voice is seductive, not bossy. His teeth nip my inner thigh, and I yelp. Then his tongue swirls over the same spot he bit, and it feels amazing. "Now you're going to find out what it's like to be punished by me."

"Oh yeah?" I say because this is what we do. We spar. Back and forth in our verbal tennis match. "What is it like?" I'm genuinely curious. Rafe punishing me? It shouldn't be hot, but my insides curl.

He starts to stand. I try to push his shoulders back down, but it's no use. The guy is like a truck. That smile is on his face again, which thrills me more than anything. He's like a different person when he smiles—even more devastatingly handsome but also youthful and open.

"I should turn you over my knee." His big hands glide over my skin to my bottom, and squeeze. Hard.

"So why don't you?" I challenge. I try to sound coy, but my voice comes out eager. Breathy.

He scoops under my knees and carries me to the bed where he lowers me to my feet and spins me around.

A strangled giggle comes out of my mouth as he pushes my torso down over the bed and slaps my ass.

I jerk at the shock of contact, but he immediately massages the sting away. "Mmm."

Maybe this was what I was resisting about Rafe being the boss of me. This sexual dominance that leaves me shivery and soft.

Surrendered.

Maybe I knew on some level how much I'd love it because I want it so badly now it terrifies me. I don't like to be needy with anyone. Especially not a guy like Rafe.

He slaps my ass again, a crisp, business-like smack that makes me cream my panties. After he rubs away the sting, he slips his fingers into the waistband of my panties and jerks outward, ripping them. "I'll replace these." He tosses the ruined panties away.

"Oh God," I murmur. Why is that so hot?

His hand rests on the back of my leg, and I gasp when he snaps one of the garter belt straps. "You can call me Sarge."

I laugh because it's too late to take offense to any of his high-handedness. This is something else now.

This is sex, pure and simple. And I love the way he plays the game.

He delivers three quick slaps, and this time, when he rubs, his fingers slide between my legs.

My pelvic floor contracts, and I almost have a mini-orgasm just from the first touch on my most sensitive parts. "Rafe," I choke.

"That's right, princess." He strokes more firmly between my legs, rolling the pad of his finger, which is slick with my juices, over my clit.

"You like that, beautiful?"

I love that he asked. He's not barking orders any more. He's listening to my body. Paying attention to my needs.

When is the last time I let anyone do that for me?

"Mmm hmm," I moan, arching my back for more. "I like your punishment."

Rafe makes that growly sound again and drops to his knees behind me. He grips my thighs and pushes them wider then uses his thumbs at the creases of my ass to part my cheeks wide and roll my hips back until my pussy meets his tongue.

I cry out at the delicious contact. Rafe doesn't hold back. He laps at my juices like a starving man, his tongue firm and direct. He penetrates me, then rolls it over my clit. "Rafe."

I read once that men—and women, for that matter—love to hear their name called out during sex. I didn't have that in mind when I moaned his name, but his response is swift and obvious. His touch grows rougher where he holds my cheeks and thighs apart, and his tongue whips over my lady bits then all the way back to my anus.

"Oh my God! Rafe!" I'm shocked by the contact and unbelievably pleasured. I want more, yet I squirm to get away, as if the mounting orgasm is something to fear.

"Rafe… Rafe. *Rafe!*" I come all over his tongue, my pussy clenching on air, my legs shivering against his palms. He keeps on licking until I'm spent, then he stands and slides an arm under my belly, scooping me onto the bed on my back.

He climbs over me with heavy lids and a smug smirk on his soft lips. "I guess you're pretty satisfied with yourself." It comes out more like a purr than a barb, and I reach for him to soften any offense.

"I thought you were the one who was pretty satisfied," he murmurs back, kissing me with his lips still glossy from my juices.

I work the button on his jeans, grateful his torso is already gloriously naked. "Almost," I murmur. It's not true, I'm already more satisfied than I've ever been with a man, but I want more. We've come this far, I need the whole Rafe package.

"You want this?" He shucks his jeans and boxers. His cock springs out, thick and hard. Straining in my direction.

"Yes."

He produces a condom from the nightstand without my having to ask. Of course, Rafe would be responsible. That's his gig.

I take it from him and rip it open. What can I say? I have control issues, too. "Come here." My voice has never sounded so husky in my life. Rafe walks on his knees until I can grip the base of his cock, holding it steady. I sit up and take him into my mouth, giving him a thorough sucking before I roll the condom over his wet cock. The shudder that runs through his body makes me feel as smug as he looked a moment ago.

Rafe lowers his mouth to my right breast, sucking on my nipple, but I'm too impatient for more foreplay.

"Uh uh," I say, pushing his head away. "I need you inside of me."

Rafe lifts his head, his gaze amused. Indulgent, even. "You're still fighting me for dominance, aren't you, beautiful?"

With that, he rolls me to my belly and gives my ass another slap. I don't mind because I promptly feel the nudge of his cock between my legs. "Yessss," I hiss in pleasure then grunt when he thrusts in deep. He stops at the hilt and ripples of shock and pleasure spiral out from my core. "You okay?"

"Little late to be asking, isn't it?" I snark, but there's no bite to it because it feels absolutely wonderful to be filled by Rafe.

He punishes me by not moving.

I wiggle my ass.

"You want this cock, princess?"

I try to push back, taking him even deeper than he's already seated. "I want it," I admit.

He lets out a rumble of satisfaction and eases back to push in again.

I whimper at the pure deliciousness of it. "Yes, that," I encourage.

"You want to get fucked by me?" He's taunting me now, but I don't care because when he pins both my forearms to the bed, my body becomes a live wire, trembling, needy, desperate for his next move.

"You like to be held down, hmm?" I don't know how he knew it, but he's right. My pussy gushed the moment he restricted my movements. "You only surrender to an alpha?"

I would try to sort through his statement, but I can't because he's moving inside me, sending tidal waves of pleasure crashing through me with each perfect stroke.

"Let go, princess. I'll give you what you need." He increases the force of his thrusts.

My brain scrambles. "Yes," I babble, not meaning to say anything at all. But it's too late, it's like the cork is out, and I'm spilling my truth everywhere. "This is what I need. This is exactly what I need."

"Fuck, yes," Rafe exalts behind me, thrusting with more vigor, his loins slapping against my ass. "I'll give it to you," he promises in the same uncorked babble-tone I had.

"Can you come on demand, Adele?" he asks, surging behind me, driving me wild.

I don't understand the question, so I can't answer. I'm pretty sure my brain checked out the moment he started undressing me.

"Hmm?"

All I can do is buck against him, show him how badly I want it. How much more I need.

"When I say now, I want you to come for me. Do you understand?"

My mouth opens on a silent cry. I'm so close.

"*Now*, Adele," he commands.

My body obeys like a runner released by the starting gun. The climax uncoils in a wild release, sending me catapulting into outer space, my eyes rolling back in my head, my face buried in the covers.

Dimly, I'm aware of Rafe's shout and his beautiful finish, timed perfectly with mine. He continues to ride me, to ride out the orgasms until he's moving in slow undulations, stroking my insides like a love song. Like a tender caress.

His lips find my shoulder, then the back of my neck. He releases my arms and brushes my curls to one side to kiss along my jaw. "You're so beautiful, Adele. So glorious."

~

Rafe

"Y-you're glorious, too," Adele pants.

I push away the crowding awareness that I'd had the urge to mark her. That what my pack brothers have been pointing out is true.

Adele is my mate. I can't unpack that, just like I couldn't let my wolf off-leash to claim her. I'm in no position to mate. I'm the alpha of a mercenary shifter-ops pack that engages in the most dangerous missions invented.

Adele, this incredible, talented, feisty, gorgeous female, is a human. Fragile. Delicate. If I mated her, we could have children instead of pups. They, too, would be fragile. I can't live knowing someone I love could be ripped from my life again. I won't live that way.

It's simply too much to bear. Fearing for her safety tonight was bad enough.

"Are you going to let me take care of you now?" I can't stop myself from getting bossy again.

She rolls over on the bed and blinks up at me with her cinnamon-shadowed eyes.

"What was that fight about? With Channing and then Deke? You acted crazy."

"Did I scare you?" I murmur. "Princess, I would never hurt you."

She huffs. "I know that. But you wanted to hurt them."

I shrug. I can't explain pack dynamics to her. "Just letting off steam."

She rolls her eyes but lets it go, muttering something about "macho men" and "too much meat."

I stroke my thumb down her cheek. "You scared me tonight."

"Did you lose someone?"

I suck in my breath, drawing back. It takes me a moment to find my voice, and when I do, the words come out sounding rusty. Haunted. "What makes you say that?"

"Is that why you work so hard to keep everyone around you safe and managed?"

I let out the air in my lungs with a puff. "I don't know how you could know that."

She shrugs. "You were special ops in the military. It's not hard to fathom you might have lost brothers-in-arms."

She's right. I've seen combat. There have been human casualties that still haunt me. "True."

She tilts her head, studying me in the dark. "There was a specific trauma."

I'm surprised at her perceptiveness. I haven't seen it

85

before because we've always been at odds. When she was giving me sass and baiting me, there was no place for vulnerability. Maybe that's why we both like sparring so much. It's a form of self-protection.

I crawl off her and dispose of the condom.

She doesn't move, like she's waiting for my answer.

The room is dark. Probably too dark for her to see me well, which helps. I return to the bed and lie down beside her, trailing my fingertips lightly over the soft plane of her belly. She's still wearing her sexy ensemble, except for the panties I tore off her—I'll keep those as a souvenir.

Having her close is balm on a half healed wound. Her presence helps me continue.

"We lost our parents," I admit. "Lance and I. They were…" I hesitate, not wanting to expose Adele to the gruesome story. "…killed."

Her breath hitches, and she rolls into me, molding her body against mine.

I want to tell her more, even though I've never told this to a human before. The words spill out of me like a confession, "They were murdered. Lance and I found their bodies."

Adele gasps. "Oh my God. I'm so sorry, Rafe. How old were you?"

I squeeze my eyes shut. *My parent's bodies, red gashes—the wounds opened by their attackers—marking their faces and hands…* "I was fifteen. Lance was eleven. I kept us together in foster care until I could get custody of him. That's why I went into the military—to provide for him." It wasn't human foster care—another pack took us in, but I still had to fight to keep Lance and I together. He was the only family I had left.

Adele strokes her hand over my shoulder and down my

arm. "That's a huge trauma. I can see how it would leave a big mark."

I grunt. I never considered my need to keep those around me safe a sign of dysfunction—a scar in action. I mean, I'm alpha. It's literally my duty to protect the pack. But the idea of not having this constant life-or-death seizing around my heart makes my eyes burn.

Like some alternate me—a healthier, healed version, might be filled with peace and power rather than trauma and the need for the most brutal revenge.

"I've been seeking closure for a long time," I rasp into the darkness.

"Closure…I'm guessing that doesn't mean a lot of therapy to help you forgive."

"No. It means revenge." Closure means the slow, painful death of whoever killed our parents. The memory of Gabriel Dieter dangling that information rises to the surface and makes me grit my teeth. Does he really know who killed them? Was it him? I intend to hunt that man–or whatever he is–down and find out. "I want justice."

"My mémère used to say that you don't need closure with anybody but yourself. That's the true secret to power."

"Mmm." I'm too satisfied from watching my mate come to openly disagree.

Her laugh is low and husky. "I know, I never subscribed to it, either. But what if you could just be your own closure? Let yourself off the hook for seeking revenge. Stop hanging onto that event and letting it continue to shape your life."

I'm suddenly bone tired. The weight of needing to protect everyone in my life and avenge my parents has caught up to me. There's been so much death in my life. All the ghosts of my past swim before my eyes. My fallen brothers-in-arms. The men, human men, who served with me and died by my side. My parents. I failed them. I couldn't save them. I couldn't protect them. The shifters in my ops pack are mine to lead and protect. To keep alive.

"Just let me fix your tires."

Adele hesitates, and I think she's going to keep making me crazy, but she agrees. "Okay, but you're taking the cost out of my wages, assuming I still have a job."

"You still have a job. So long as you stop flirting with Channing."

She lets out a sleepy laugh. "You are ridiculous. Why don't you just try flirting, yourself?"

"I prefer making you mad."

"Ridiculous," she murmurs, but her breath has deepened, and she drifts off to sleep in my arms.

Fuck. I don't know how I'll make it through the night with her in my bed.

Rafe

"So did you mark her?"

Channing's big dumb face is ridiculously eager when I walk into the garage at six a.m. Even Deke looks up from where he's working on replacing Adele's tires.

I rub my face. I couldn't sleep last night trying to keep my wolf on leash. This morning, I was out of bed by five. If I stayed and watched Adele sleep, I'd end up fucking her again. And probably mark her. That's the last thing I need to do.

I needed to get away from Adele, and I didn't have the heart to wake her. She's still sleeping in my bed.

Where she should be, my wolf points out smugly.

"No," I answer shortly. "Of course not. I'm not going to mark Adele or claim her as a mate." I emphasize this with a kick to a piece of metal that happens to be in my way—the stupid 'art sculpture'. It goes spinning out of the open garage door and bounces off the pavement onto the lawn.

"Easy." Channing raises his hands. He and Deke

exchange glances as if silently consigning themselves to walking on eggshells around me.

"She is your mate, though?" Deke asks.

I fold my arms across my chest. "You wanna talk about this? Share our feelings?"

"Absolutely." Deke puts down his wrench and mirrors my position. "If she's your mate—and it's obvious she is—then you've got to claim her."

Yes! My wolf shouts.

"No."

"You don't have a choice," Deke points out. "You're an alpha wolf. You'll go moon mad."

Fuck, Deke's right. Channing is crouched behind Adele's car, replacing her tires and removing himself from the conversation at the same time. Smart. My wolf doesn't see Deke as a threat because he's already mated.

"I can't do it."

"So let's review the options." Deke holds up a finger. "Worse case, you go moon mad. Completely nuts. And you're so dominant, it'll take all of us to take you out. That means we might get hurt. "

"It's not going to come to that." Even I can hear the lie in my voice.

Deke holds up a second finger. "Lance has a new mate. They're expecting a baby. You go crazy, we have to put you down. That means a fight to the death. You could hurt or kill your brother, and his baby grows up without the protection and support of a father."

"Fuck," I mutter, and Deke nods in agreement. He knows he's twisting the knife. I want to pummel his face, but I stay where I am. Deke's right, and I deserve to hear this. I deserve the pain.

"Best case, you stay on edge, growing more miserable with each passing month," Deke says. "We got a taste of that last night. You'll be even more of an asshole than you already are." He shrugs. "You might make it a year or two before you go moon mad, and we have to kill you."

"I'll leave before that happens."

"You won't be in your right mind. Your wolf will take over and drive you crazy. And I care about you too much to watch that happen when there's an easy solution: Claim Adele."

"You're chatty this morning," I mutter.

"I have a mate now," Deke snaps. "I don't fuck around. Question is, why are you?"

"Oooh." Channing pops his head up over the car. "Mic drop."

"Shut up," Deke and I say at the same time. He and I glare at each other, arms still folded across our chests. After a minute, Deke's eyes flash, showing me his wolf, but he drops his gaze, respecting my dominance.

"I can't claim her." I turn away. Images crowd my mind: my dead parents, lying on the floor of our home. My brother Lance's bloodless face. He was just a kid, and I was a teenager when we lost everything. The need for revenge that has haunted me every day since.

I can't go through that again. I won't.

"Sarge?" Channing calls, and breaks me out of my reverie.

"Do a full detail after you replace the tires," I order. "When Adele wakes up and comes down, give her her car and let her go home."

"You gonna be here?" Deke asks.

"Nope." I ignore the anguished howl of my wolf. "Going on patrol." A thirty mile run should get some of my restless energy out. At the very least, it'll get me away from here. Far away from Adele is where I need to be.

~

ADELE

"So how's the new gig going?" Tabitha asks as we leave the coffee shop. I shove my hands deeper in my pockets.

"Um, good," I lie. I have no idea how the new gig is. I've spent the past twenty-four hours trying not to think about it.

Two nights ago, I slept with Rafe. Was it only a few days ago I was gazing longingly up the stairs to Rafe's bedroom and wondering if he slept naked? Now I know. He sleeps in the buff, his whole delicious body laid out like a buffet feast for the eyes.

But then he leaves the bed before dawn. Not only did I wake up in his bed alone, he didn't even wait to see me off. Deke was waiting with my car keys.

On one hand, my truck was completely detailed, down to the new tires. That was nice.

On the other, *Rafe fucking left.* I had to gather up my things and walk out of the lodge in front of everyone in my day-old clothes and *no panties*—the ones he ripped were nowhere to be found. Of course, everyone knew I'd spent the whole night in Rafe's room, and that he left before I woke up.

Talk about a walk of shame.

Deke and Channing made some lame excuse about how Rafe has a lot of work this week. I didn't see him at all yesterday when I dropped off lunch and made dinner. I fumed the whole time, banging pots and pans, searing his porkchop until it was over-done and burning the top of his creme brulee. A few days of working for Rafe, and I could write a whole cookbook on passive aggressive baking.

He did replace the panties he ripped—in a classic asshole Rafe way. Last night, the dick *emailed me a gift card to a lingerie shop.* I nearly emailed back telling him to go fuck himself.

The only reason I haven't quit is because I need the work. The salary Rafe promised is filling my bank account nicely. A few more payments, and I'll have an installment payment to give the landlord.

Tabitha tosses away her empty cup in a public trash can and falls into step beside me. "You sound so excited," she observes. "C'mon, you wanted to meet for coffee without Charlie and Sadie for a reason. Talk to me."

"It's not that I don't want to talk to Charlie and Sadie." Both of them know about my night with Rafe by now. "They're not going to judge me, but–"

"They're both in happy, healthy relationships. I saw Charlie and Lance picking out baby clothes the other day. It was so adorable, it hurt," Tabitha says with a twinkle in her eye that tells me she's joking. "I actually got cramps in my ovaries. And then they went into overdrive, and I nearly mounted the mailman. The one with the comb-over and bad teeth."

"Oh my God, same," I laugh. "I love how they are together, but when I went with Charlie to pick out paint colors for the nursery, I almost bought a can of baby blue and some wallpaper decorated with tiny elephants."

"I know, right?" Tabitha squeals, and we both giggle. Already my chest feels lighter. Meeting with T was a good idea. "My uterus is dialing my brain, asking when I'm going to give my mom grandbabies."

"Doesn't your mom call and ask you that?"

"No." Tabitha grimaces. "She asks if she can set me up with some weak-chinned, New York City hedge fund billionaire. And when I refuse, she laments that I quit my modeling career. According to her, the fashion runway afterparties in Milan are the best way to meet a sugar daddy–my term, not hers." She hooks her arm through mine as we cross the street. "What about your mom? Does she drop hints about who you're bringing home for the holidays?"

"No. My parents still want me to go to med school and become a doctor like them."

"What about your business?"

"They don't believe in my business dreams." Mémère was the only one. "But I've got a chance to make it work." I tell her about Rafe's job offer and the high salary he's paying me.

"Alrighty then," Tabitha says after a pause. "So what's the problem?"

"It's Rafe. He's an asshole. He's also…"

"Really, really fine?" my friend says with a devilish grin.

"Tabitha!"

"What? I can't look? He is."

"He is." I bite my lip. "And we…" I can't say it. I catch her eye and blush.

"Oh, I see." Tabitha holds out a fist to bump mine. "Get it, girl."

"It's not that simple." The whole story comes rushing out.

"He left?" Tabitha practically shrieks.

"Yes…but…" I find myself wanting to explain more. To defend Rafe. "He told me things…" I hesitate because I don't want to share Rafe's business. "He opened up to me, Tabitha. He told me about his childhood, how he took care of his brother, why he joined the military."

"Then he ran."

"Yes."

"Like the scared man-boy that he is."

"He's not a man-boy. He's all man. He's been through a lot, Tabitha. I don't want to share deets, but let's just say he has suffered a lot of trauma. A lot. And getting close to someone probably triggers him."

"Sounds like he has relationship PTSD."

"Exactly."

"Well, I'm not one to judge, either. But boss/employee relationships…"

"I know. Bad idea."

"I might have a little trauma of my own, watching my mom seduce her bosses. Her married bosses."

"Yikes." We walk another block in silence.

"So what are you going to do?" Tabitha asks.

"I don't know. I like this job." Do I get another job? Can I get another one as good?

"If you keep the job, what are you going to do about Rafe?"

"I don't know that either." Do I forgive Rafe and ignore him? Can I ignore him? "I don't regret sleeping with him." For a little time, he'd taken my mind completely off the mess of my life.

"You can always catsit," Tabitha swings her long, straight hair out of her face. "That's what I do when funds get low."

"No thanks, I'll leave that to you." Tabitha has a carefree spirit, and I've never known her to hold a traditional job. She pays her bills through a combo of selling her craft art and cat sitting and dresses in the groovy vintage fashions she finds at estate sales and fixes up.

This afternoon she's in bell bottom jeans and a crop top under her vintage coat, and her outfit manages to be fashion forward in the most retro way possible. Tabitha always has good timing. If she wanted she could sell her clothing creations online and build a big business, but when I mentioned it to her years ago she wrinkled her nose and told me all that work didn't sound like a good time.

"Aren't you cold? I'm freezing." I rub my hands together.

"Not really." She shrugs. Her coat's hanging open. "I'm hot blooded." She digs in her oversized macrame bag and pulls out a scarf. "Here. Early Christmas present. I knitted it myself."

"Thank you." The scarf is a classic cappuccino color that will match everything I own. Tabitha loops it over my head, and it settles around my neck like a cloud. "My God, is this cashmere?" I finger the soft fringe.

"Yeah, I had the wool leftover from a sweater I made to order." Tabitha twitches the scarf this way and that, nodding and stepping back when she's styled it to her satisfaction. "You'd be doing me a favor. It doesn't go with any of my clothes."

"Well, thank you. What do the holidays hold for you? You going to see your mom?"

Tabitha grimaces. "God no. She's in the Seychelles until February. I'm going on a road trip down to a jewelry convention in Texas. Have a few estate sales to hit on the way there and back. So if you call me and it goes straight to voicemail, just know I'm in the canyon."

We hug and Tabitha lopes off. I continue on towards the plaza.

I quicken my steps. I'm passing by the cobblestone alley that leads to The Chocolatier, but I don't want to see it the way it is, the windows dark and a closed sign on the door. I want to imagine my shop brightly lit, full of happy people.

What did Mémère always say? *Hold a picture in your mind of what you want. Do not think of the problem; picture the solution.*

My mémère would visualize the business she wanted to build, even when she was young and penniless. She told me how she'd stand on the sidewalk in front of the building that would become her boarding house. She imagined the front door swinging open with people coming and going talking and laughing paying their bills. She imagined herself living a long life with her wealth growing. Rings on her fingers and emerald bracelets on her arms. And she built a successful business that supported her family. Even after she sold the boarding house, she had funds to pay for all my mother's college and med school and live in style. *No man gave me this,* she'd say, fingering a diamond ring. She funded all her grandkids' college, and we still all got an inheritance when she died.

The seed money for my shop came from that inheritance. *I'm sorry, Mémère. I'm going to lose it, and I don't know what to do.*

If she were here now, Mémère would smile and straighten her diamond ring, her emerald bracelet. *You've lost nothing, cher. Out of nothing, a way can be made. Reality follows you. Show it the way.*

I have a few minutes before I'm supposed to meet Sadie for Christmas shopping.

I stop next to a snow covered flower bed and close my eyes. *Hold a picture in your mind of what you want.* The Chocolatier appears in my mind's eye–the window and door clean and polished to a sheen, smiling customers flowing in and out, each one carrying a white bag or two. Carrying the scent of caramel and chocolate on their winter coats. Carrying a bit of warmth and love in the form of chocolate creme and sugar dusted truffles.

When I open my eyes, I've got a big grin on my face. This is working!

I continue down the sidewalk, letting my dream unfurl. Happy customers, happy shop, happy landlord. Money piling up in my bank account. New clothes–silk and satin, lingerie from my favorite boutiques. Handcrafted lace next to my skin, enough to drive Rafe mad…

And he appears instantly, dark hair tousled, dark eyes drawing me in, the side of his mouth tipped up in a cocksure smile. His body flexes, six feet something of insane muscle. There's a little line of dark hair trailing from his navel down into his black cargo pants. And then his pants disappear…

Sweet baby Jesus. I stop short and put a hand to my chest. *No, no, no, Mémère. That is not what I want.* He left me yesterday morning. He didn't even stick around to hand me my keys.

He doesn't want me, which upsets me. But what's more annoying is—why is he being the sensible one? I'm supposed to be the one pushing him away, so I can keep my cushy job and get back to my shop.

The shop. That's what all this is for. I don't need a freaking man.

I close my eyes and try again to hold a picture in my mind of what I want, but all I see is Rafe without a shirt or pants.

Goddammit! "Get out of my head, naked Rafe," I mutter.

"What?" someone behind me growls, and I leap about fifteen feet into the air. I whirl to find Rafe's right behind me, his hands grabbing my coat to steady me. How can a man so big move so quietly?

"Nothing," I say crisply. "What are you doing here? Were you stalking me?"

"If I were stalking you, you wouldn't notice," he purrs, and my heart flips over. "I'm here to meet Deke, and I saw you from across the street. You looked like you were having a heart attack."

"Women have very different heart attack symptoms than men," I snap because I'm still mad at him. "It's not always chest pains—" I shut my mouth because why am I arguing with Rafe about the symptoms of a heart attack in the middle of the plaza? What I really want to do is slap him then break down and ask why he left. Where he's been the last two days.

His hand closes over mine, and my heart threatens to flutter out of my chest. "All right, princess," he soothes. "If it wasn't a heart attack, then what was it?"

A Rafe attack. But, no, I can't tell him that.

I flip Tabitha's gift scarf over my shoulder. Rafe hovers so close, the tasseled end hits him in the face. Oops. "Nothing," I say, trying to gather the scattered shards of my dignity. I guess we're not going to talk about our night together. Fine. "I'm fine." I go to take a step, and my heel hits an icy patch, and my leg goes out from under me.

I hit the solid wall of Rafe's body and end up in his arms, slanted across him like we're tango dancers posing for a song's finale.

"You're wearing boots again." He scowls at the high heels. "How do you walk in the snow with those things?"

"Elegantly." *Except when you're around.*

He sets me on my feet, and I make a fuss out of straightening my clothes. After a moment, he brushes my hands aside and starts adjusting my coat for me.

"You better start wearing something practical, princess. I'm not always going to be behind you to catch you when you fall," he says in that rough voice of his, his patented sexpot growl. Every word sends goosebumps over my skin.

I had a snappy retort on the top of my tongue, but one look into his face, and it flew away.

He's looking at me like I'm a cupcake and good enough to eat.

His hands are still on my coat, and I feel their warmth penetrate all my layers of clothes straight to my skin.

He hums, and he adjusts my scarf in a careful way that

makes me feel like he wants to tear off all my clothes. "This is nice." He rubs the scarf between his thumb and forefinger, and I feel the ghost of his touch between my legs.

"Tabitha gave it to me." I lick my lips. "Why do you call me that?"

"Call you what?"

"Princess."

"Because you're high maintenance."

"Is that so?" Lord, this man makes me want to rip his head off his shoulders every time he opens his mouth. If Mémère were here, she'd say it's because I really want to rip off his clothes.

I'm glad that Mémère isn't here to see her favorite granddaughter making a fool of herself over a man.

"I'm not high maintenance," I say. "I just look good. I like to look put together. Besides, what does it matter?" I add with a little French shrug. "You're not the one maintaining me."

He cocks his head. "That's right. I just get to enjoy the results." There's a flash of light in his eyes. His gaze warms me through and through.

Rafe looks leaner somehow, the hollows of his cheeks deeper, his cheekbones sharper. There's a forest of shadows beneath his eyes. His dark hair falls over his face, and my hand itches to brush it back. He's been keeping long work hours, and it looks like he's been missing sleep.

My first instinct is to ask if he's been eating, and order him to sit, so I can feed him. Heap his plate high and sit close to him to make sure he finishes it. And then climb in his lap and straddle him to give him his reward...

I blink. Where the hell did that thought come from?

But now he's staring at me, looking straight into my eyes.

"Where's your winter coat?" I make a show of looking around for it. "It's freezing out here."

He's in his usual black henley and a vest. His tan cheeks are chapped. He's not even wearing a hat. I can see the heat from his body escaping out the top of his head.

"Worried about me?" His eyes are smoldering.

"You think *my* clothes aren't practical…"

There's a flash of green light from his eyes. But I must be seeing something. Maybe the Christmas lights reflected or something weird.

"Let me see something." I grab his arm and step in front of him to study his eyes for a moment.

"What are you looking for, princess?" His voice is even more gravely than normal. He crowds into my space again, and I don't hate it.

I shake my head. "It must be a trick of the light. Sometimes your eyes look green, but they're actually…" my voice trails off.

Our lips are a few inches apart.

"What, princess?" his breath wafts over my face.

"Dark brown…" I swallow. We're close enough to kiss, and my body is burning up. I tug the scarf away from my throat. *My goodness.* I wave a hand in my face while Rafe looks at me like I'm nuts. It's freezing out here, and suddenly I'm too hot for my coat.

"Adele…"

"Full moon tonight," I say desperately, turning away and continuing to trot down the sidewalk. "Or not tonight, but in a few days. Soon."

"Yeah." He falls into step beside me, looking amused, like he knows what I'm doing. *Distract. Deflect.*

"Did you know the word *lunatic* actually comes from the word *luna* because it was believed that the moon caught madness intermittent insanity?" I keep babbling. "My mémère told me about moonlit nights in New Orleans. People act crazy…well, crazier than normal."

His brow furrows. "What are you trying to say, princess?"

I was going to say something about women's menstruation cycling with the moon, but that's probably taking the distract and deflect tactic too far. "Oh, nothing. Just making conversation."

He steps in front of me, making me stop short.

"Is this about the last time we were together?" he murmurs. "You and me, my bedroom. You gonna plead temporary insanity?"

I guess we are going to talk about this. "No. I knew what I was doing. And I liked it." I hold my breath, waiting for his answer.

"So did I."

Warmth curls through me. "But—"

"It's probably not a good idea to continue," he finishes the thought for me.

"No." Why am I so disappointed? "I like my job, and I want to keep it. Screwing the boss is never a good idea. But we can be friends, right?"

He looks almost pained. I hate seeing him in pain.

"Truce?" I stick out my hand.

He raises his chin and closes his hand around mine. For a moment, he just holds it. My breath catches, but then he shakes it firmly. "Truce."

"Adele!" someone calls.

I drop Rafe's hand and step away.

Sadie and Deke are up ahead. My friend's cheeks are chapped with cold under her bright red hat. Deke strolls beside her, taking one long stride for two and a half of hers.

I wave back to my friend and hasten toward her. Rafe

sticks to my side, his fingertips brushing the small of my back. He's barely touching me, but I feel it in my whole body for the rest of the night—his hand hovering in the small of my back, ready to catch me if I fall.

∽

THE STRANGER

It's been so long since he's walked among the commoners. In this new age, men and women mingle together freely. Children are allowed to run and play and laugh loudly.

He stands in the Taos plaza and observes. He has not lived such a long life that he is not good at observing.

Since he awoke, everything has changed. The world is modern, made new. But people are still the same. The peasants still gather in the square. They shop and talk and greet one another. The main difference is that coffee is no longer something to sit and savor for hours—it's poured into little paper cups and carried everywhere.

He came to the high mesa following Lightfoot. Normally he wouldn't lower himself to personally chase after a quarry, but his kind always enjoys playing, as a cat plays with the mouse. It's food.

He spots his quarry across the plaza. A big man, Rafe Lightfoot. Almost boring, duty bound.

Not the most interesting diversion but better than nothing. He adjusts the dark glasses he wears to hide his eyes and starts to cross the street. No use being close to the enemy and not letting Rafe know he's here, in the wolf's territory. Taunting the enemy is the best part of the game.

And then he catches a ribbon of scent, and his foot hovers in midair. No, it couldn't be. It is impossible.

After years of searching the seven continents, there she is—right in front of him. The one female in the whole world who belongs to him. His mate.

"Adele," her friend calls, and the lovely female waves back.

Adele, *that was her name. It would take but a moment to dart out and grab her and swoop away.*

These puny humans would scatter as soon as they saw his monster. The two wolves would fight, but they would be no match to him.

But the whole snatch-and-grab maneuver lacked a certain style. He considers himself a gentleman. A mate must be courted and wooed. What use was all the treasure he'd amassed, if he could not display his vast riches and awe his true mate?

Adele, he murmurs to himself, tasting the name like a drop of honey on the tongue.

And there she is… with Lightfoot. The wolf hovers over her, crowding close. Acting protective of the female Adele. Acting almost like his wolf claimed her as his mate.

Well, well, a conundrum.

His enemy suddenly became that much more interesting. Mayhap that's what drew him to stalk the wolf in the first place.

"To the contest, then," he mutters and smiles. He would go and gather his resources in preparation to woo Adele. She would be safe with Lightfoot. And it would give him time enough to arrange a display of his immense wealth and all he has to offer a mate.

It will be easy to win the female. Lightfoot cannot compare.

Adele would come to him. Choose him.

If not, then he would burn the whole world to ash and lay it at her feet.

8

Rafe

A pig roast.

The female is driving me mad.

That's nothing new, but each day that passes having her enter and leave our compound without my sinking my teeth into her shoulder to forever claim her as mine makes me more and more aggressive, more on edge.

I swear, despite her agreeing that we can't be a couple, Adele is trying to drive me insane. Today it's a pig roast, or as she called it, *cochon de lait*. A taunt at me for insisting she serve more meat.

It means she's been here since early morning pit roasting three pigs. The entire property smells of delicious, mouth-watering meat, and it's drawing prey animals to our territory. I had to growl at a pack of coyotes slinking through the trees, and now I just caught the scent of an opportunistic bobcat.

I scan the boulders to locate it. A twitch of an ear betrays its presence beside an outcropping. "Go home," I toss out. "We're not sharing." I glance up in the sky at a circling hawk. "Not with you, either."

I've been patrolling along the property all day. I can't very well leave Adele unattended out here where there are wild animals lurking. This is exactly the reason I can't claim her. My need to keep her safe is a widening pit of terror inside me.

It's hard to imagine anything that could soothe it, and taking her as my mate would have to intensify that need. An alpha wolf protects his own female and pups over all else.

Fuck.

Without asking me, unconsciously—or perhaps consciously—taking the role of female alpha, Adele issued invites to guests of her own choosing for the pig roast. I've monitored their arrival from afar, not trusting myself to be civil to anyone in my current state.

But then I hear the sultry notes of Adele's voice, and the irrational rage over her flirting with Channing sends my boots crunching through the snow at a run. Before I arrive, Channing gives a piercing whistle in two short bursts, a non-urgent signal to gather.

Food is ready. It's late afternoon, and the sun is just setting. I don't mind an early dinner.

I slow my run and draw a couple deep breaths. There will be civilians present. I need to act like a fucking human not a wolf on the brink of moon madness.

I stop at the glass sliding doors, catching my breath at the sight of Adele holding court in my castle. She's in another one of those Goddamn dresses—as beautiful as they are impractical. This one is emerald, with cut-outs at the shoulders and across the chest to show her gleaming brown skin. Her hair cascades in a waterfall of curls across her shoulders, a matching emerald strip of fabric holding it back from her face. The color brings out the green in her hazel eyes.

When I step in and take a plate to serve myself from the steaming heaps of meat and vegetables, Adele's lips curl in a satisfied smile, like she knows how badly she's torturing me. It makes me want to carry her off to my bedroom and spank that gorgeous ass red again.

...and that thought gets me so hard, I have to turn away and adjust myself.

"Smells delicious," I mutter when I walk up to her with my plate piled high.

She gives an exaggerated gasp, her fingertips on her chest. "Did you just pay me a compliment?"

"Your cooking is fine." I try not to look at her because just standing this close has me sweating. Her scent wraps around me like a warm embrace, dragging me under.

"Just fine?" She puts her hands on her hips and purses her pouty lips.

"It's good," I admit. "It's..." –I can't tear my gaze away from her mouth– "...perfect."

A layer of protection slides off her, and she relaxes. "You *do* like it, then?"

I want to punch my own face for making her believe I didn't. Have I really been such an ass? I already know the answer.

I mold my palm lightly around her upper arm and lower my head. I don't know what confidence I was about to spill–that her food is as taunting and tempting as she is? That I'm refusing the deliciousness of it because I'm afraid it will ruin all other food for me? That she ensnared me with her skills the first time I set foot in The Chocolatier? Whatever it was, I'm spared from the confession because Lance interrupts.

"Important message from Kylie. She needs you to call her right away."

Thank fate. An excuse to retreat before I blow Operation Avoid Adele. I give Adele a curt nod and carry my plate into my office where I sit down and call Kylie, a cat shifter from Tucson who is probably the world's best hacker. We subcontract work to her on a regular basis because her mate is a wolf, and we trust them both.

"What's up, Kylie?"

"I've been monitoring the dark web for the situation with Charlie and Adele, and something popped up."

A steel band squeezes around my chest. Last month, Charlie, my brother's mate, was kidnapped when some drug dealers mistook her for Adele after Adele's business partner, Bing, got himself into trouble dealing drugs and then got himself dead.

"What is it?" I choke.

"The drug cartel thinks Adele has Bing's drugs. They put out a capture order."

Adrenaline hits so fast, I almost shift. I flush with heat, and my vision changes for a moment. I don't know if or how I ended the call to Kylie, all I know is my need to protect my mate sends me barreling out of my office to find her.

"I need a plane out of Taos by 1800 hours," I bark at Lance.

"Who will be on it?" he clips back, pulling out his cell phone.

"Me and Adele."

His posture relaxes like he thinks I'm taking her on a honeymoon, which makes me want to pick him up by the throat and shake him. "She's being hunted by the cartel," I snarl.

He snaps back into urgency, putting the phone to his

ear, presumably calling Teddy, the bear shifter who we use as our pilot.

Adele stands frozen in front of the stove, her green eyes wide. "What did you say?"

"They think you have Bing's drugs. I'm moving you out." I take hold of her elbow. "Come on, let's go."

"Wait, I can't just–"

"I'll clean up, Adele," Sadie offers quickly.

"Yes, we'll get it." Charlie agrees, rubbing her baby bump. "You go. Let Rafe handle it."

ADELE

The assumption that Rafe should swoop in and save me rankles. I guess it's a result of the same pride that keeps me from accepting help from friends. I want to be able to handle problems on my own.

On the other hand, I'm certainly no match for a drug cartel if they're hunting me.

I take my coat from Rafe and follow him out to his Humvee. "Where are we going?"

"Out of state." He throws open the passenger door for me and practically lifts me inside. Jeez, the guy is strong. Like, crazy strong. I don't know how that was even possible. "Somewhere we can lie low until I can take care of the cartel." He buckles my seat belt and slams the door shut.

"How are you going to take care of the cartel?" I ask when he climbs in the passenger side.

When he looks at me, his eyes flash with green light, and for a moment, he reminds me of a ferocious animal. I'm reminded of the fact that this man probably kills for a living.

A shiver runs up my spine. I definitely wouldn't want to

be on the wrong side of Rafe and his team. My initial irritation with Rafe's high-handedness slips away, replaced by gratitude at his willingness to protect me.

"Thank you," I say quietly, folding my trembling fingers together to quiet them.

Rafe has already peeled out, and we're driving swiftly down the mountain. He looks over at me, his brows down, his gaze troubled. "I won't let anything happen to you, Adele," he swears, and I believe him.

For the first time in ages, it occurs to me that I don't have to do everything by myself. I can let people help out when they offer. But then again, it was letting Bing help me open The Chocolatier that now has my life in danger. And I don't know what Rafe will want in return.

Actually, that thought doesn't ring true.

Rafe isn't the kind of guy who asks for things in return. He's not transactional. He functions from a sense of honor and duty. He would protect anyone in his sphere. Of that, I'm certain.

I reach out and touch his forearm, which is corded up like he's in a wrestling match with the steering wheel. "I'm glad you're in my corner."

"Always," he swears, like it's a given. Even though we're not a couple. Even though he hasn't known me all that long, and most of our interactions have been combative. He gives me that blazing gaze again. "I will never let anyone hurt you," he says fiercely.

I'm reminded of how he opened up the night we had sex, and I feel the need to remind him, "It wouldn't be your fault if someone did."

I meant the words to be comforting, but if anything, they seem to further enrage him. His lips draw back from his teeth like he's ready to kill anyone who hurt me.

"Rafe." I stroke up and down his arm. "I just don't want to be your responsibility."

He sucks in a sharp breath, and then a sense of quiet power settles over him as he exhales. "Protecting you is what I have to do." He holds up a hand to stop my protest. "Wait. Let me finish. It's a compulsion, Adele. But it's also an honor."

"Wow." I clear my throat. I don't know what I've done to earn Rafe's respect, but I suddenly feel safer and more cared for than I ever have in my life. "Thank you. Really."

Rafe takes us to the tiny Taos airport and parks. He spots a small plane he must recognize because he takes my hand and pulls me toward it at a jog.

I'm in my heeled boots and a thin-strapped, lacy bra that offers little support to my boobs, so running isn't my best look. "Hold up," I shout.

Instead of slowing, Rafe pivots, scoops me up in his arms and runs carrying me, like he did that night I slid off the road. I have to admit, it feels nice to be carried.

I can almost see Mémère nodding smugly. Like she orchestrated all this as my guardian angel to show me how supported I am.

That I don't have to do it all alone, even though that's what she chose.

We get in the plane, and Rafe takes the time to strap me in. The pilot is a huge guy with a military buzzcut. He gives me a thumbs up and a grin.

"Where are we going?" I ask again because his vague answer last time didn't satisfy me. "I know you're used to your team following you blindly, but I'd like to know where you're taking me."

"We have a ski lodge in Utah. They shouldn't be able to find you there."

~

"Whoa. You own this place?" I ask.

"Sorta. We bought it via a conglomerate with a few friends of ours."

Rafe unlocks the front door to what he called a "ski lodge" but is in actuality a mansion. The floors are pale gleaming wood, polished to a marble-like shine, and the building stretches out in all directions. The living room features a fireplace suspended in the center of the room, with another wall of windows like Rafe's place in Taos. Clearly he has a thing for bringing the wilderness indoors.

Some military-looking guy met us on the tarmac in Utah and handed Rafe a set of keys to a Jeep. And we drove another hour into the mountains to get here.

"Friends?" I ask, gaping at the vaulted ceilings. "Are they here? Is this where they live?"

"Nah. They have their own place in Tucson. It'll just be us."

It occurs to me that Rafe is some kind of multi-millionaire, which seems at odds for how hard he works and serious he seems. Like, why have this incredible ski lodge if he can never let his hair down? It's hard to imagine him even knowing how to enjoy it.

The lodge is beautiful. Like their Taos compound, the construction and furnishings are expensive without being ornate. Functional, but with all the nicest amenities.

Rafe heads into the kitchen carrying a large cooler that could probably be rolled. I walk to the windows, only to find it's actually a retractable wall. It's dark out, but the moon is full, lighting the snowy forest. Steam comes from around the corner. I unlatch the wall and push it open a crack to step outside and investigate.

"Don't go out there in those boots!" Rafe barks from

the kitchen where he's unloading the cooler of groceries that apparently came with the vehicle. "It could be icy."

I roll my eyes and ignore him, shutting the door to his voice. The air is freezing, but it's too beautiful to mind. I find the source of the steam in a huge natural-looking hot tub set beneath two boulders as if it were a hot spring pool in the wild. I drag the cover back and turn on the jets, which sends a cascade of water down the boulders in a hot waterfall.

It's glorious. Totally inviting.

I'm not sure whether I want to torture or reward Rafe when I decide to strip out of my clothes and climb in. The hot water shocks my chilly skin, but it feels so good. I moan softly as I sink up to my shoulders, my curls trailing into the water.

"Adele?" Rafe's sharp voice barks into the crisp night.

I sigh, wishing for once he wouldn't be so on edge. We're in a different state. Far away from the drug cartel. I'm safe. I'd like to see Rafe unwind. Find out what he's really like. What's his real personality under the gruff sargeant exterior?

"Right here," I say softly.

"What are you—" He comes around the corner and freezes the moment he catches sight of me. His gaze trails over my boots, coat and scattered clothes on the deck then back to me in the water. He picks up my bra and rubs it between his fingers like it's a mink stole, and I suddenly wish I'd let him take it off me the way he did last time. I love that he appreciates my lingerie as much as I do.

"It looked too inviting to pass up."

Rafe's eyes gleam in the darkness. "I—" he chokes out. "You—"

I arch a brow, not bothering to hide my smile at what I've done to him. "What's wrong, Rafe?"

"You can't be out here alone—*naked*."

"Oh, I think it'll be fine. You said it'll just be us, right?"

"It's not safe," he grits out.

"You're here with me, right?"

He looks around, scanning the darkness as if he can see into it. For a moment, I'm sorry for tormenting him because I can see how seriously he's taking protecting me. Maybe it's not about my nudity, and he truly is worried about my safety. Now I need to know for sure. Or maybe I just want it to be the former. I rise up a bit in the water, giving him a view of my breasts. "Would you feel better if you came in with me?"

I'm definitely playing seductress—something I shouldn't do. Something I decided was a bad idea. But the need to help Rafe relax overrides my better judgment.

"No!" he sputters, but he stalks forward with purpose. He's either going to join me or pull me out. I'm not sure he knows which it is yet.

"Rafe." Speaking his name makes his gaze lock on mine, his focus clear. "Come in."

His nostrils flare as he sucks in a breath, and then I know I've won because without breaking our gaze, he strips out of his clothes and drops into the water, his cock standing straight out.

I've never had such an effect on a man before. It's a powerful feeling to know he's so attracted to me. No less powerful than my attraction to him though. I rise to my feet and meet him in the middle of the pool, my mouth catching his at the same time my wet breasts glide across his firm chest.

He moans against my lips, like our every touch is torture. Maybe it is because I suddenly can't get enough. I loop my arms around my neck and press my body against his, feeling the prod of his erection against my belly.

He makes a desperate sound, his tongue sliding between my lips, his hands kneading my ass in the water.

My body comes alive everywhere I'm in contact with him, like he's waking my cells from slumber. I suddenly have no idea why I've been resisting this thing with Rafe. It would be madness not to give in. I can't imagine having this kind of chemistry with anyone else on the planet. He backs me up against the stonewall of the hottub. "Adele," he murmurs between rough kisses. "I need to get you out of this soaking pool."

I break the kiss and raise my brows. "You really think it's dangerous here?"

He pulls me back into him. "*I'm* dangerous. To you. I need you on a softer surface."

I laugh against his lips as he climbs out and carries me inside, leaving our clothes out on the deck.

He carries me into a bedroom with a giant king bed in the middle and another hanging fireplace near the window with two comfy sitting chairs. With the flip of a switch, the flames in the fireplace springs to life.

Rafe drops me in the center of the bed and begins to kiss down my body, starting at my collar bone and traveling down my breastbone then the plane of my belly, stopping at the apex of my sex. "I don't have a condom," he admits in a gravelly voice.

Rafe

Claim her.

My wolf has only one desire. The moon is full, and I'm way too on edge to be touching Adele, but it's impossible to stop.

"It's okay, I'm on the pill, and I'm clean. I haven't been with anyone but you in more than a year."

"Thank fuck." Ack, did I say that out loud? Well, the sentiment is true. Not being inside Adele would kill me at this point. "I'm clean, too."

Claim her.

I lick into her, re-familiarizing myself with her soft folds, the tang of her essence. Her skin is still hot and wet from the soaking pool, which makes me all the more driven to claim her. Like she's one of her delectable entrees, fresh out of the oven.

I swirl my tongue around her clit until it lengthens enough for me to get my lips around it and suck. She cries out, filling the room with the sweetest sound.

With every beat of my heart, I sense the rushing up of fate to tear at my heels. To force me to claim her.

But I haven't managed to protect my team and my pack this long without a fuck-ton of discipline. I can do this.

I can satisfy my female without claiming her.

Claim her.

My wolf needs to back the fuck down. This is for Adele, not me. I can't claim her. I already drive her mad with my need to protect her, and we're not in a relationship.

This is for Adele, I silently chant as I crawl up over her and drag my cock through her juices. I thrust into her, and she arches up with a gasp.

I force myself to stop. "Too much?"

"No," she pants, gripping my shoulders. When her nails score my skin, I surge inside her, trying to hold back from ramming home like her sweet cunt might save my life.

Maybe it will. I close my eyes and force my movements to be slow and steady.

I ignore the crumbling of walls all around me. Inside me. The changing of my very essence simply by blending with hers. I move inside her, and she rocks to meet my thrusts, a perfect dance. I brace my hands on the head-board above her, keeping my fangs far from her sweet moonlit skin. Every sound she makes drives me more mad, but I somehow manage to hang onto a thread of control. I watch her tension build, listen to the pitch of her cries raise. She is beauty and ecstasy. She is everything I've been missing. She is life itself.

She shrieks when she comes. Wraps those long legs around my back and holds me in. I fill her with my essence, and I think that alone is what keeps me from sinking my teeth into her perfect flesh and forever claiming her as mine. My wolf is mollified that I've marked her with my cum. Left my scent all over her, at least temporarily.

As soon as we both have finished, I drag myself off her to get control. In the bathroom, my wolf eyes look back at me from the mirror, a greedy green.

Claim her.

I shake my head at my reflection, dragging in slow breaths until my eyes change back to brown. Even then, I don't dare return to her.

ADELE

So much for not screwing the boss.

Rafe disappears to the bathroom after sex while I revel in the glorious aftermath. My body is well-sated. Last time wasn't just a fluke. I can now confirm with all certainty that my chemistry with Rafe is off the charts good.

And now that I understand better what makes him tick—that his control issues and overprotectiveness stem from the trauma of his parent's murder–I only have compassion for him. His bossiness is him trying to keep everyone he cares about safe. And I get the feeling that even though he's already accepted me into the fold–one more of his flock to keep safe–he's afraid to let me in.

He's suffered too much loss to want to risk it all.

I climb out of the bed and check the drawers, finding one with a stack of neatly folded white t-shirts. I pull one over my head and go in search of Rafe.

I find him standing in his boxer briefs in the kitchen, holding two full glasses of water.

"Hey," he says softly, extending one glass to me. I accept it and drink. "Are you hungry? Did you get to eat before we left?"

"Yes. Did you?"

"Not enough." He casts a baleful glance at the refrigerator. "I wish to hell I'd brought your feast with us."

I shrug. "I'm here." I meant that I could cook more, but his eyes glint, and his expression grows hungry, as if the sex we just had wasn't nearly enough for him.

"I've figured out all our issues," I tell him.

He lifts his brows. "Oh yeah? What are they?"

"Your parents' death makes you overprotective, and my parent's lack of assistance makes me not want to accept help. We're a recipe for conflict."

He steps into my space, his hand coming to rest lightly on my hip. "Your parents didn't help you?"

"It's not that. They loved me. I had everything I needed growing up. But they didn't support my dreams. They wanted me to be a doctor like them. They think what I'm doing is a step down. The only person who ever supported me was my mémère. I opened the Chocolatier with the inheritance she left me. I was working hard trying to prove they were wrong, but…"

Rafe's brows slash down. "Oh you'll get your shop back," he says fiercely. "That thing with Bing–that wasn't your fault. You know that, don't you?"

"I'm the idiot who partnered with a guy with a drug habit."

"Ah. Another reason not to accept help now, right?"

I offer a rueful smile. "That's probably true." The weight on my chest descends, though, thinking about what I need to get The Chocolatier back open. "Working for you is a help," I tell him. "I didn't realize Bing hadn't been paying the rent, so I'm in arrears. The landlord won't let me back in until I pay it off."

Rafe doesn't look surprised. "How much do you owe?"

"Ten thousand. So I figured if I could stick out a month of working for you, I could get back to it." I wince a bit, thinking he will be offended, but there's something indulgent about the way he's looking at me.

I go still. "Wait... did you know all this already?"

He tips his head to the side studying me.

"Is that why you offered me the job?"

When he doesn't immediately answer, I know I'm right. The proud part of me is pissed off, but it's drowned out by gratitude. I don't know why Rafe took an interest in me, but I can deny how good it feels to be seen. To be cared for.

Loved.

Rafe lowers his forehead to mine. His lips are so close it's hard to concentrate. "So..." His voice has a coaxing lilt to it, and the hand on my hip has slid inside the hem of the long t-shirt. "Now that you've identified our issues, are you going to let me help?"

"I'm still here, aren't I?"

His grin turns wicked. "As if you had a choice."

I try to push against his rock solid chest, but he goes nowhere.

He captures me by banding an arm behind my back and pulling my body up against his. "I'll help you get it open. Will you let me?"

My breath catches in my throat. My instinct is to say no, but that's just my habit. To put up barricades and refuse anything that's not an even trade. Rafe's eyes crinkle with amusement as he watches my struggle.

"Maybe," I say finally.

He lets out a chuff of laughter before he brushes his lips across mine. "Accepting help isn't a weakness. It's a strength. Don't be weird about this."

I try to give him another playful shove away. "You calling me weird? This from the guy who strips off his shirt to wrestle his subordinates in the snow during dinner. That's ripe."

"That's not weird," he says, but there's laughter on his face, and I love how youthful it makes him look. "That's normal for us. I guess it would seem weird to you. I'm sorry it made you uncomfortable. I have a hard time staying rational around you."

I want to take it as a compliment, but Rafe seems to sober, as if he doesn't like his reaction to me. But I guess for a guy who craves control, falling in love might feel like skidding across black ice in an old truck with bald tires.

It feels that way a little bit to me, anyway, and I don't have half the control issues he does. I reach out and interlace my fingers with his. I want to tell him that I'm falling in love, but I know that would make whatever internal struggle he's having harder, so instead, I lead him back to the bedroom, ready for another round.

9

Rafe

I get up early to shift and run because staying in bed with Adele last night had me half feral and awake most of the night. I pleasured her twice more before we slept, and watching her come might be the highlight of my entire life.

Maybe I should claim her. The guys are right. I can't go on this way much longer–it will end in disaster. Best case, it actually kills me. Worst case, I hurt Adele or someone else I love.

Yes, I love her. Shifters don't think in terms of love. Mating is more biological to us, yet I'm starting to understand what humans must feel. It goes beyond physical attraction. It's the need to just be near her. To listen to the sound of her voice, to learn the complexities of what makes her so special.

I find our clothing still out on the deck, frozen to the wood planks, and it turns me half-feral again, wondering what Adele's wearing right now. I gather the clothes, groaning aloud over her bra and panty set–another sexy duet, this time in navy and white polkadots. When I step inside, I pull on some clothes and drop our frozen ones in the washing machine. Then I follow my nose to the kitchen where I find Adele wearing nothing but my t-shirt again.

She's made the space her own, moving around like she's boss. It's a given that my dick is hard, but my mouth also waters from the smells coming from the oven, and there's something less physical and more all-encompassing that wends its way around me, binding me to her with invisible cords.

"Smells delicious. What are you making?"

Adele tosses a sexy smile over her shoulder at me. "Sausage, mushroom and spinach frittata." Her eyes rake up and down my body. I'm in a pair of sweatpants and a t-shirt, but the way her gaze heats, she must find me enticing. Does the human mate of a shifter recognize her mate's scent on some level? "Did you work up an appetite?"

"I'm always hungry around you," I admit in a rough voice. I grip her nape and lift her face to mine for a searing kiss.

Her lips kick up into a smile when I break it. "Five minutes." She bites my chest through my t-shirt.

"I'll take a quick shower," I tell her. "I put our clothes in the washing machine. Not that I want you to put any on."

If I could somehow keep and hold forever the smile she sends me, I would. It lights up my insides like a wildfire, demolishing every resistance in its path.

Why haven't I claimed her?

Because losing her would kill me, I remind myself.

But not having her is killing me, too.

Lance calls as I'm about to get into the shower. I consider not answering, but I'm the alpha. I can't ignore my pack members.

"What's up?" I growl into the phone.

"We're moving in on the cartel," Lance says.

"What? Not without me you're not."

Lance makes a dismissing *pfft* sound. "We don't need you. They're just human. We found out where they operate. They have a mansion outside Santa Fe. Channing, Deke, and I are driving down right now. We'll take care of it. You keep your mate safe until we've eliminated the threat."

"Negative. Wait for my command. I repeat—"

Lance ends the call.

Sonofabitch.

I call him back, and the fucker sends it to voicemail. I am seriously going to kill him for breaking the chain of command. Even as I rage, I recognize what he's doing. My pack is trying to take care of me for a change. I can't stand it—just like Adele can't stand letting me take care of her. Yet accepting help is as much a gift as offering it. Every time Adele allows me to help her, it soothes my wolf. Maybe it's not exactly the same for my pack—they aren't my mates—but I can see how they might want to do this for me.

For us.

Just like I'd do anything for them.

I grit my teeth and climb in the shower. I'm sure they can handle themselves. They're well-trained and nearly invincible. They definitely know what they're doing. Still, something niggles in the back of my mind. Something doesn't feel right about any of this.

THE STRANGER

They threatened his mate. These petty criminals high on their own dust. The minute the alert went out on the dark web channels his hackers haunted, he knew she was in danger. His eyes slitted, and his spine vibrated with the advent of the monster.

No one threatened his mate and lived.

It took a few hours for his hunters to find the cartel headquarters. Another day to deliberate the cartel's end. He had an army at his beck and call, but why should they get the pleasure of destroying the damned? Of razing the cartel's compound to the ground? The cartel threatened his mate. This was personal, and called for a personal solution.

There was a monster inside of him. It was time to let him out.

The flight to the cartel's headquarters was easy. He took off from a nearby helipad, and a few minutes later hovered over their mansion. The air whipped over his face, scented with aspen and pine–tinder for the coming fire. As he drew closer, the wind blew the lawn furniture askew. Atop the roof, the stone chimney trembled.

He took a brief moment to savor the cartel's destruction. A deep inhale, and then… the cleansing flame.

It was the work of a moment. He did not wield a weapon, he was *the weapon. Like conquests of old: the targets knew his wrath and glorious power a second before they died, consumed in fire.*

After the first pass, the screams of the dying seasoned the air. Gray smoke billowed from the remains of the enemy's mansion, like incense rising from a priest's censer.

Another pass, and gusts of wind flattened the lawn grass, tore down trees, fanned the rapidly spreading flames. He was patient, he was thorough. His flame carved a path through the cartel's mansion, turning the center into an inferno. Blue fire incinerated the wood and cracked the stone. Turning sand to glass. Turning the mansion and the living beings within to charcoal and ash.

And then: blissful, holy silence, broken only by the beating wind. The epicenter of his destruction was a blackened hole. Triumph!

He'd extinguished the enemy's lives as quickly as snuffing a candle. The threat to Adele was gone, and he was the one to obliterate it. Not the Alpha wolf who thought to protect her. They were late to the hunt. *There was no living thing left for the wolf pack to kill. They would find that soon enough.*

The wailing sirens of the human emergency vehicles echoed up to the clouds. Soon the world would know what would happen to anyone who dared threaten his beloved. And the wolf shifter who dared to think Adele was his? Lightfoot would soon know the truth.

She is mine!

He would protect Adele. She belonged to him, not the wolf. Lightfoot had served his purpose: instinct had told him to hunt the wolf, and instinct had been right. The wolf Lightfoot had led to Adele. After years of searching, he'd finally found the only woman in the world for him. He'd been patient, bided his time to learn more about her, so he could woo her properly, following the rituals of his people. But now there was no time.

WIth the cartel gone, only one obstacle remained in his way—the wolf pack. And they would be distracted by this sudden move by a hither-to-unseen player. While they were scurrying around on the ground like ants around a ruined hill, he would fly to Utah. With Rafe gone, the way would be clear to meet Adele.

The destruction of the cartel served two purposes: to remove the threat to Adele and remove her pesky Alpha wolf bodyguard from her vicinity. One move: two satisfying outcomes. That was how he played the game.

The taste of smoke lingered in his mouth as he turned for the final leg of his flight.

It was time to meet and claim his mate.

ADELE

After breakfast and another mind-blowing round in the sheets with Rafe, his phone rings. His brow furrows as he lunges for it on the nightstand.

"You fucker," he says when he picks it up. "You hang

up on me again and–*what?*" Rafe flies out of the bed. I hear the loud, brusque tones of someone on the other line–Lance, I think.

"Who killed them? What? I can't hear y–*fuck!*" Rafe keeps his back to me as he hunches over his phone. "Lance? You're breaking up. What is it?" He curses again and brings the phone in front of his face. I hear a ringtone on speaker that goes straight to voicemail. *"Fuck, fuck fuck!"* he chants.

"What is it?" I ask.

When he turns his eyes have that weird glow to them. "I have to go." He yanks on a pair of jeans that he grabs from a drawer.

"What? Okay, but what's happening?"

"It's the cartel. Lance and the guys located them and moved in this morning against my direct orders." Rafe scrubs a hand across his roughened jaw as he paces to the dresser to yank out a shirt. "The connection cut out. He said something about the cartel having been killed but that I had to get there right away. He was shouting something urgent, but I couldn't make it out."

I launch myself out of bed, too. "Okay, I can be ready in two minutes."

"Oh no." Rafe stops and points at me. "You're not going anywhere." His eyes flash with dangerous warning. "It's not safe."

I'm sure he's right, but his tone rankles. I lift my chin. "So what? I'm supposed to stay here while you–"

"That's exactly what you're going to do. You sit tight. You're safe here. No one knows about this lair. I can't be worried about you and my pack–I mean, my team–at the same time. Understand?"

I seriously want to rip his head off.

This bossy thing is beyond old.

But Rafe is half out of his mind with worry. Tense lines bracket his mouth, and the muscles of his neck and back stand out in stark relief as he pulls his t-shirt over his head. "This was a mistake," he's muttering. His eyes flash green as he looks right at me. "I can't deal with distractions."

Well, excuse me. I didn't realize I was a distraction. I cross my arms over my chest. If I hug myself tight enough, I can hold my cracked heart together.

He finishes dressing and steps close. His shadow falls over me, and my arms quiver, wanting to wrap around his waist. "I'll be back as soon as I can. I'll call you when I know more. Keep the doors locked. Do not leave this lodge–not even to go in the soaking pool."

I glare at him.

His lips thin. "Promise me."

"Fine."

"Thank you." The relief in his voice is evident and makes me feel better about giving into him when he's being such a jerk. He gives me a hard kiss then whirls and marches out.

Rafe

TEDDY FLIES me to an airport in Santa Fe, and we drive out to the last address I have on my packmates' phones. I still haven't been able to reach any of them. Teddy takes the wheel while I stay on my phone, trying to call them, and grip the oh-shit handle so hard I leave a palm print on it.

Lance had yelled something about the cartel having been brutally savaged and then, "Oh my fucking God, you won't believe this," but that was all I could get other than

"Rafe—come here." The fact that he still hasn't been in communication scares the crap out of me.

"How you doin', man?" Teddy glances over at me. My jaw tightens, and I scroll through my phone one more time, refreshing to check for messages. Nothing.

There's a crack, and I'm holding the pieces of the oh-shit handle in my hand. I roll down the window and hurl them out.

If anything happened to Lance, I'll never forgive myself. Adele is a fucking distraction—I lost all focus with her, and this time it may have cost me my team. This is my punishment for thinking I could have a mate. I can't have a mate.

I can never have a mate.

"Almost there," Teddy mutters. And my phone comes alive in my hand, beeping with notifications. A dozen texts from Lance, but I don't have time to read them because Teddy is cursing and telling me to look. Ahead of us is a barrier of two fire trucks and several military vehicles. They're blocking the road, their flashing lights washing over the wreckage of what used to be the cartel's mansion.

It looks like a bomb went off. No, not a bomb but some sort of fire. The scent of smoke hovers in the air. The center of the building is gone. There's a blackened hole where the house used to be. Scorch marks bloom over the crumbling outer walls. Everything's charred but in a strange pattern.

Colonel Johnson stands on the lawn, feet planted and hands on his hips. Lance and the guys are with him.

Thank fuck.

My fear morphs into fury as I stride over.

"What are you doing here?" Lance asks, as if he hadn't called me yelling two hours ago. "I said *don't* come here.

Don't come here! What the hell are you doing? Where's Adele?"

I splutter, about to launch into a tirade, but Colonel Johnson thrusts a manila folder in my hand. "It was your boy Gabriel Dieter. Look what he left you."

I shoot a startled look at Lance who nods at the folder. I flip it open. Inside is a dossier on our family. Of Lance and me, in particular. Our ages, lineage, stats. The address where we'd lived. Where our parents had been murdered.

My hand shakes as I turn the pages. "Wh-what is this?"

"Looks like it had something to do with your parents' death." Colonel Johnson meets my gaze. "They were hunting young shifters."

"Who?" I roar. I'm going to kill them. Every last one of them. I will have my revenge if it's the last fucking thing I do.

"It doesn't say."

"You think Dieter left this?" I flip the folder over and see the message written in… fates–it looks like it was written with an old-fashioned quill pen. In a neat, loopy script are the words,

ALPHA RAFE,
> *Want revenge? Give up my mate.*
> *–G. D.*

ADELE

I'm not upset, I tell myself as I pace back and forth through the house. *It's fine.*

I'm not mad Rafe rushed back to his home to do his mission and help his brother. And there's no reason for me to be worried. His work is dangerous, but he can handle it. He's an adrenaline type person. I keep imagining him on his missions, as cool and in control as he is in normal, everyday life. Delivering commands like he's ordering a burger.

Of course, in my daydreams, he's never wearing more than camo fatigues and work boots. Maybe he has a bullet bandolier strapped across his chest, aka Rambo-style, but mostly he's just topless, his awesome pecs and abs flexed and flecked with sweat. Every muscle on him honed to perfection by Mission Impossible stunts, necessity rather than vanity at the gym.

It makes my nether parts very happy when I replay this image over and over in my mind. It's almost enough to keep me from stress baking three different types of Christmas cookies.

Almost.

No, I'm not mad that he went on a mission. I'm not even mad at what he said in the heat of the moment. *I can't deal with distractions.* Not the nicest thing anyone's ever said to me, but I get it. During the mission, worrying about me will be a distraction.

What does upset me is that he's treated me like a distraction from the beginning. I can deal with his high-handedness and our constant sparring matches, but what rankles, deep down, is how Rafe is constantly hot and cold. He pulls me close, only to thrust me away. He doesn't really want me in his life.

We're like magnets, drawn to each other in one moment, repelling each other in the next.

After eating my weight in raw cookie dough, I pace the house and end up downstairs, passing the indoor sport court, the massage room with the Himalayan salt wall, the 8-bed bunk room, and the bowling alley. This mansion is so luxe it's nuts. It'd be fun to be snowed in here all winter–if I were with Rafe. The chillaxed, non-secretive version of Rafe. I know that Rafe exists, I've caught glimpses of him. Intense but not stressed. Dominant, but not overbearing.

We were so in sync before, the absence of him hurts.

I heave a sigh and head out of the ski locker room to the outdoor patio. I know Rafe said to stay inside, but I'm too restless to be cooped up, and he's way too controlling. The snow-covered world looks so beautiful. If the cartel were here, wouldn't they be more likely to find me in the house versus in the woods?

Out on the patio, the sandstone tiles are somehow magically clear of snow. Must be heated. *Fancy.* There's even a walkway of sorts, leading into the woods, and even though I'm in my impractical high-heeled boots, I feel like taking an easy hike. I head down the path, my hands tucked deep in pockets.

The snowy forest is beautiful–as flawless and magical as a landscape captured in a snow globe. I follow the path through the trees, frowning at nothing and no one, blowing smoke into the frosty air.

The path forks, and I head to the left, following ski tracks. My boot prints will help me find my way back. Rafe told me the owners of the mansion chose it because of easy access to a ski resort. Apparently they can ski to the lift and back.

After a few minutes of walking, I hear the whir of the ski lift and see the slopes angling down to the side. Wow, the ski mansion really does have a prime location.

In front of the lift is a warming lodge. It looks like a tea house, built out of red wood and rows of windows in a Japanese style. There are plenty of ski tracks leading up the stairs.

It looks so inviting I have to step inside. I push the

door open and find a roaring fire with comfy chairs angled around it. The inside is even more charming. The air is toasty warm, my face thaws a little and my shoulders relax.

Everything in the place is ready to host an elaborate tea, including the sideboard holding a few tiered cookie holders filled with tea biscuits. In the center of the table is a stunningly elaborate copper teapot sitting atop a rounded bulb base. A samovar, used in places like Russian and Turkey. The teapot is hot, as if waiting for a guest to come take tea. I lean over the cunning contraception, sniffing the extra rich spiced brew.

Who heated the tea pot? The place is empty. There's no staff or any guests, only the ski tracks and a few boot prints leading up the steps and back down.

It would be wonderful to take tea here. It's so warm, and everything is neat and cleverly designed in the small space. Beyond the windows, a few sparse snowflakes fall. I stand for a moment, taking it in.

"Oh hello," a polite voice murmurs. "Are you here for tea as well?"

I whirl, taking in the tall man in a dark coat standing a few feet beyond the door. He's wearing thick sunglasses that remind me of Stevie Wonder's. Maybe he's partially blind.

"Um." I glance down at the table. It is set for tea. Duh, that's why the samovar is heated and the tiered trays are filled with biscuits. "No, this isn't for me..." my words die as he removes the sunglasses, revealing dark eyes and thick lashes.

My mouth falls open. The man is stunningly handsome, with sharp cheekbones and an aquiline nose. His head is uncovered, and his dark hair shines under a light dusting of snow. He's still standing outside of the tea house, down a few steps. It puts our heads at the same level.

"I, uh, I…" My cheeks heat. This must be a private rental, which means I'm intruding. "I just wanted to see the tea house. It looked so warm."

"Yes, it is quite cold out. There is a bit of a snowfall at this moment." His voice has a touch of an accent, but I can't place it. "Were you skiing?" he asks with a smile. His canines are a little pointed but his smile is charming.

"No, I'm staying in one of the houses nearby, actually."

"Ah, then we are neighbors," he exclaims. "Forgive me, I am new to the area. I have not met many people."

"I'm only staying here temporarily," I say. "At a home that belongs to friends of…my friend." I suppose Rafe can still be considered a friend, when he's not being an ass.

"My house is back there." The man gives a casual wave in the direction beyond the trees. "But like you, I adore this tea house. As soon as I saw it, I said 'I must have tea here.'"

"Yes, I don't blame you. I feel the same way." I should probably go and leave him to it, but before I can say this he nods to the table.

"Do you like the samovar? It is my own."

"This is yours? It's beautiful."

"And the tea is ready. Chef Giampi is very proud of his creations." He steps into the tea house, slowly unwinding his cream-colored scarf. He smells delicious, like expensive cologne. Although I prefer Rafe's rugged good looks, woodsy scent and a day's worth of scruff, I can still appreciate a gorgeous man when I see one. "Please, you must stay and have tea." His voice rings out with that compelling command Rafe sometimes has, except his tone isn't barky like Rafe's—it's silky.

It's bizarre.

"Oh, no, I couldn't intrude," I protest, yet my body is already complying with his request, walking toward the table.

"It is no intrusion." he declares. "Please. The chef made far too much for one person, as his *nonna* taught him to do." He lays a large hand on his chest and bows a little. "Please, madam. You would do me great honor."

"All right," I say, my heart skipping. I feel a little light-headed. Something about this man is magnetic. Powerful. For some reason, I want to gush to my friends about him. Sadie and Charlie are happy in their relationships, but Tabitha is single, and this guy is fine. I could see her with a guy like this. Out of the ordinary, like her.

"Please," he says again, waving to a chair, and I find myself stepping forward.

"Excellent." He swoops behind me and pulls out my chair. Before I know it, he's served the tea and raises his cup to mine in toast. "To neighbors. Ms..."

"Fabre. Adele Fabre. Please, call me Adele."

"Adele." His voice is rich and warm as a cognac. He takes my hand and bends over it like we're in an old-fashioned movie, but instead of kissing my hand, he inhales deeply. When he lifts his head, there's a slight line between his brows, but he says smoothly, "A pleasure to meet you. I am Gabriel Dieter."

Rafe

As soon as Teddy touched down, I tore out of the helicopter. Now I'm in the Jeep, zooming up the switchbacks, taking each turn on two wheels.

I can't reach Adele. She left the house. She disobeyed me.

And deep down, my wolf thinks it's my fault. I don't know what game Dieter's playing, but my wolf instincts tell me to get back to Adele. ASAP.

I never should've left.

I try to call her cell and the house, taking the next turn with only one hand on the wheel. Nothing.

Fuck!

My phone buzzes, and I answer. It's Lance—who's been texting me since I read the note and raced out of the scene of destruction.

"Did you reach her?" he asks by way of greeting.

"Not yet."

"I contacted Kylie," he says. "There are cameras all through that house—she had turned them off for privacy but just did a scan. No heat signatures in the house."

Fuck!

"The note—we're pretty sure it is from Gabriel Dieter. But what the fuck is it about? Is he a shifter?" Lance muses. "Does he have a mate?"

"It would make sense." I round another curve, gritting my teeth like it'll keep me on the road. "He knew silver bullets would hurt me. He has inside knowledge somehow."

"What I don't get is how he thinks Adele is *his* mate. I thought she was yours…" he trails off, and I hate the hesitation in his voice.

"She *is* mine," I growl so loudly the cab shakes. My eyes have to be bright green right now.

A pause. "Have you claimed her?"

"No."

Fuck.

I can't have a mate.

My wolf howls, and I grip the steering wheel. I need to

135

get in control. It's reinforced, but I've ripped them off before.

"Let us know what you need. Lance out."

I toss my phone in the seat beside me and focus on the road. I would drive off the side of the mountain and into the snowy forest if I thought it would help me reach her faster.

I told her not to leave the damn house. But it's my fault for leaving her. *Never again.*

I've got to keep Adele safe.

I'm coming, Adele.

ADELE

The winter wind has picked up. It blows a layer of snow off the drifts. The temperature is dropping, but inside the tea house, I'm warm and cozy. "So you live close to here?" I ask my host, Mr. Dieter. *Gabriel,* as he insists I call him.

"I have a house, yes. A recent acquisition. Everyone said I must have a place in Park City, so…" He waves a casual hand as if to say, *so I bought a mansion. No biggie.*

Meaning Gabriel is not only model-hot, he's also rich. I file this away to tell my friends. Tabitha's weird about rich guys, probably because her mom is always trying to set her up with shystie stock brokers, but this guy is so charming.

He's removed his gloves and coat but replaced his dark glasses. "Do excuse me," he says as he does. "My eyes—the light."

"Of course." No wonder his glasses look prescriptive, he needs them.

"Park City's supposed to be really cute," I say.

"You have not seen the little town?"

"No, I'm under house arrest," I joke and add quickly, "I'm kidding." *Sorta.*

He cocks his head, but he doesn't seem alarmed. "House arrest can be fun," he says lightly. "Depending on the house."

"The house is certainly very grand." Ginormous even. "It's back that way." I wave behind me. "The modern style home, with its own watchtower." And a freaking bowling alley–but that might not be uncommon around here. Maybe all the mansions come with their own bowling alleys.

After a cup of steaming tea, I've grown warm enough to shed a few layers, too. I shrug off my coat but leave the scarf Tabitha gave me, loosening it and draping it just so about my shoulders, the way my mémère always wore hers.

"That is a lovely scarf." Gabriel says as he sets a cookie tray closer to me. "Do you mind if I inspect it?"

I frown. Inspect it? Okay, this guy is definitely a little weird. Still, I can't see any harm in it, so I unwind the scarf and hand it to him. He brings it to his nose and inhales. "What a beautiful scent. How disappointing it's not yours."

This guy is definitely a little strange.

"Oh, is there a scent? It must be my friend Tabitha's perfume. She gave it to me."

"Tabitha," he murmurs. "Lovely name."

Time for some not-so-subtle probing. "The name 'Dieter' is German, correct?"

"And 'Fabre' is French. Although you can never tell if someone is actually French or German by their last name. This America was populated by all sorts, as I have found. I'm new to the country as well, as I'm sure you can tell. My accent holds me apart."

"No, no," I rush to say. "Your English is very good."

Gabriel sits back, toasting me with his tea. "I am from many places. I've had a long and varied life. Right now my favorite home is in *Italia*. *Lario*. You would say Lake Como. You know it?"

"Lake Como," I repeat. "Yes. "

"Have you been there?" he perks up.

"Uh, no." I nibble a tea biscuit to buy me some time to remember what I know of Lake Como. Wasn't a recent James Bond movie set in a mansion there? "I've heard it's very nice."

"Oh yes, you must visit."

"I think my friend Tabitha actually has been there."

He leans forward. "Has she?" He brings the scarf to his nose again. "That would make sense."

"What do you mean?"

"It is of no matter." He adjusts his glasses.

A dark shape between the trees makes me start. Gabriel's head whips around.

A man clad all in black marches up to the tea house, stopping in front of the steps. He doesn't look like a resort staff member, even though the black military pants and black flak jacket looks like a uniform of sorts. "Sir," he says with a crisp nod.

"Ah, excuse me," Gabriel says to me, rising and giving me a small bow. "I must confer with my employee. A small matter."

"Of course."

Gabriel bundles up again and heads outside to speak to his employee. I pretend to ignore the two men's conversation, but can't help hearing the rapid waterfall of Gabriel's commanding voice. He speaks another language, but it doesn't sound like German. Maybe a dialect? Definitely not Italian.

I eat two more bites of cookie and crumble the rest

onto my plate. Gabriel ends the mostly one-sided conversation with a series of what sounds like strict commands.

I smile up at him as he returns and gives another bow. "Forgive me for the interruption."

"It's all right. I should probably get back to the house."

He sails to my side and pulls out my chair. He even holds up my jacket for me to easily shrug into it.

"I shall walk you home," he announces, taking up his gloves and coming to my side. He sweeps out a hand. "Shall we?"

There's no reason to refuse, so I head back down the path, and he falls into step beside me.

When we come to the fork of the path, I slow my steps. "This is where I got turned around." I admit. "I expected to find the ski lift."

"It's that way." He gestures, and we continue down the proper path, following my boot prints.

Something occurs to me. "That tea house… was it part of the ski mountain?" I assumed it was.

"Not exactly." Dieter says. He points to a tree marked with a small pink tag I didn't notice before. "This is the boundary of my property."

"You own all this?" I blurt and recover my surprise. "It's beautiful." I'm filing away things to tell Tabitha.

"You are too kind. The place where you are staying, it is beautiful as well?"

"Definitely. It's up there." I nod to the mansion's watchtower, which we can see through the trees.

"Oh yes. The place owned by the King conglomerate. Of course. Wolf's Rest, I've heard it called."

"Wolf's Rest. That's nice. My…friend…and I are visiting while they are away." For some reason, I blush.

"A private getaway. It is very romantic, no? The snow?"

Gabriel isn't looking at me, but I get the sense that something's off. I'm not afraid, but my skin pickles.

I clear my throat. "You don't have to walk me all the way. I can find my way from here."

"Are you sure? I'd love to meet your friend. The wolf of Wolf's Rest."

"Uh," I say because I'm not sure when Rafe is getting back. And did Dieter just call Rafe a wolf?

"Let us continue," Gabriel orders, and I find myself walking ahead of him on the path. He has the same air of command Rafe does.

Am I a magnet for overbearing, yet beautiful, men? They're lucky they're so nice to look at; otherwise, I'd kick them to the snowy curb.

Which brings me back to my original problem: Rafe. My steps quicken, ready to return to him, even though I haven't figured out what I'm going to do about him.

"Adele," a voice roars, and Rafe comes racing down the path. He's not wearing a coat, and his eyes are wild.

"Ah yes," Dieter murmurs. "Here's the wolf now."

Rafe

"Adele?" My voice bounces off the vaulted ceilings when I get to the ski mansion. The place is empty.

She isn't in the kitchen and hasn't been for a while. I don't sense her presence anywhere.

I tear through the mansion, leaving a few doors askew with claw marks on the frames. Is she mad at me for leaving? I'll make it up to her. In bed. Or in the heated pool...

Outside I find the heated stone patio clear of snow, but the path beyond shows her boot prints. Even though I'm not in a coat, I plunge into the forest.

A strong scent hovers on the air. It's heavy and spicy with a smoky undertone, almost like incense. The last time I smelled it was in Gabriel Dieter's Lake Como home. Which means…

The bastard is here. Adele's in danger.

I sprint down the path and find Adele and Dieter. "Adele," I roar.

She looks unharmed, thank fuck. She starts at my shout, and Dieter's right there, taking her arm, murmuring something in her ear. My wolf goes rabid. "Get away from him." My voice is hoarse. I'm on the verge of shifting.

I need to get control. Adele can't know what I am. Once I get her away from Dieter, I need to completely distance myself from her. I can't stand her being in danger because of me. It will literally kill me.

"Rafe. This is one of the nearby neighbors, Mr. Dieter." At the same time, she steps away from him, and he lets her go.

"Please, call me Gabriel." Dieter smiles at me. There's a cruel twist of the mouth. "Mr. Lightfoot and I have met." His English is perfect, but he has a little more of an accent than he did in Lake Como.

I skid to a stop in front of them, reaching for Adele, desperate to get her safely by my side.

"You have?" Adele frowns at my high-handedness when I reach for her and pull her away from Dieter.

I insert myself between her and Dieter. My big body blocks hers from his sight. "Get the fuck out of here, Dieter."

Behind me, Adele gasps. I don't give a fuck. If Dieter pushes me, I'll go to war with him. Right here, right now.

To my shock, Dieter throws back his head and laughs.

What the fuck?

"What's so funny?"

141

"It is as I suspected," Dieter muses.

"Fuck off," I say.

"Oh, I will," he raises his gloved hands in a sign of surrender. I don't trust it. "I relinquish my claim on Adele. She's not my mate."

"Of course she's not your fucking mate!" I snarl. "I don't know what game you're playing at—"

"What do you mean, *claim on Adele?*" Adele demands. "What in the hell is going on here?"

"She doesn't even know what you are, does she?" Dieter asks, gesturing to Adele. I tense and growl, moving as if to block a blow from landing on Adele.

Dieter remains calm. "Why haven't you claimed her?" He cocks his head to the side. He's wearing black glasses, the lenses make it impossible for me to see his eyes.

A tight band closes around my throat. "She's human," I choke out, although with my wolf so close to the surface I can barely get the words out.

"What's he talking about?" Adele asks.

I need to get her out of here. "We're going back to the house," I announce, crowding her back. "We need to leave."

"No, stay," Dieter uses an alpha command, and I have to fight my body's urge to obey. What the fuck *is* this guy? "I find this infinitely interesting, wolf. After centuries of slumber, I finally have a new game to play against a worthy adversary."

Centuries of slumber... worthy adversary.

Is he a vampire? Some kind of undead?

"You have met your mate, yet you do not claim her. How long do you think you can hold off the madness?"

"I don't know what's going on," Adele raises her voice. "But I don't like this." She tries to step in front of me, but I block her again.

Dieter addresses her. "You deserve to know what he's hiding from you. Don't you want to know?"

"I don't know what you're talking about," she says in that autocratic way of hers. My princess, protecting me. "Gabriel, it was nice to meet you. *Was*. Now you need to leave." I don't like Dieter's first name on her lips, but I feel a thrill of pride at her imperious tone.

"Perhaps this is serendipitous." Dieter's still monologuing like the deranged evil nemesis he is. "For too long you've kept secrets, wolf. Now let her see the truth. You will not thank me now but perhaps at the end."

He lifts his sunglasses, and I catch a flash of weird, snakelike eyes. I don't even have time to parse the information before my wolf registers the threat, and I shift to protect Adele.

ADELE

An animal-like snarl comes from behind me. I hear the rip of clothing, and then a huge wolf leaps at Dieter, knocking him to the ground.

Rafe? I whirl to look behind me. His clothes lay in tatters in the snow.

Rafe is a wolf.

Rafe. Is a wolf.

In some kind of supernatural blast, the wolf gets thrown backward off Dieter, and the man scrambles to his feet.

The wolf's fur is pitch black with a few orangey brown markings on the tips of its ears. It surges to its feet, teeth bared. Its canines are like steak knives.

A half roar, half growl rumbles out of it, and my bones

turn liquid. Even though I know it's Rafe, I scramble back, my legs threatening to give way.

I must make a disbelieving squeak because the wolf swivels its huge head and looks at me.

"*Hold,* wolf," Dieter says in an authoritative voice. "You won't win this battle. You saw what I did to her enemies. But I relinquished my claim on your mate. She's not my intended. I won't harm her."

The fur at Rafe's nape stands up, and he lowers his head, baring his teeth again and growling.

Dieter simply turns and gives Rafe his back, sauntering away with his hands in his jacket pockets like he hadn't just been thrown on his ass by a giant wolf.

Yeah, I'm *so* not introducing that guy to Tabitha. What possessed me to have tea with him, a strange man, in the middle of a winter forest? None of my alarm bells clanged, but they're ringing off the hook now.

"R-rafe?"

The wolf won't stop growling, its green gaze fixed on Dieter's retreating back.

"Rafe."

It stops snarling and swivels its great head to look my way. He's freaking huge. His head comes up almost to my shoulder. I knew wolves were big, but damn, if I saw that thing in a dark forest I would lie down and expire on the spot. Might as well before the wolf tears me apart.

"Rafe." His name seems to be the only word I'm capable of uttering. Like if I say it enough, he'll change back into the man I thought I knew.

He lifts his mighty chin in the direction of the ski mansion, still giving me orders, even in this fearsome new form.

I wobble toward the mansion, my entire body trembling. I can't tell if I'm not breathing or if I'm hyperventilating. Either way, my lungs feel too full. Like they're going to burst.

I push open the door, and Rafe crowds me from behind, jostling me forward and then nosing the door shut.

With a shudder and crack of bones, he changes form again, into all his extremely well-built, naked glory.

"Adele."

I hear the apology in his tone, and I'm instantly mad.

Now that I recognize him I'm ready to rumble. "Adele, what?" I demand, hands on my hips.

He spreads his hands. "I'm sorry."

"You're sorry?" I echo. I stare at him, my brain still trying to put all the pieces together. "You're sorry for not telling me you're—what? A werewolf? And what the hell was that about with Gabriel?" I demand, casting a wild arm in the direction Gabriel Dieter disappeared.

"Leave him out of this," Rafe growls, and his eyes flash green.

My stomach flips as I realize what those flashes mean. They weren't a trick of the light, as I'd previously thought. They were glimpses of his wolf.

"You're a…" my breath hitches. I back into the kitchen, and Rafe follows slowly. "You turn into a wolf."

"Yes."

"Is that all?" My back hits the counter.

Rafe stops by the kitchen island and picks up the metal trash can. Holding my eyes, he crumples it into a ball, with about as much effort as it would take me to ball up a piece of tin foil.

He sets it on the marble topper, a modern art sculpture.

"All right. Okay." My spinning thoughts slow. I grab a dish towel and toss it his way. "Tell me more."

Rafe manages to get it around his waist to cover up. "Where do I start?"

"Why didn't you tell me?"

"Can't." His jaw snaps shut and clenches so hard white lines radiate over his reddened cheeks.

"I thought we were getting close."

"I wanted to, Adele. But I couldn't."

"I see." So this is why we can't be together. I'm human, and he's…not.

"So that's it, then—" I start to say when he interrupts.

"There's more. You're my…" he stops and runs a hand through his hair. The dish towel around his hips is woefully inadequate to hiding all his…impressiveness. With only his left hand holding it, the cloth is starting to slip.

Focus. I clear my throat. "I'm your what? Your mate? That's what Gabriel said. What does that mean?"

"Adele." Rafe drops his head to the side with a mournful gaze. "I can't claim you. My world is so dangerous, and you're just a human." He shakes his head. "You're so fragile. Look at the trouble I brought upon you." Now he gestures in the direction of Gabriel's exit.

But I can't focus on Gabriel. All I hear is *you're just a human.* I know Rafe's secret, and it still isn't good enough. He doesn't want me.

Deep down, I knew this from the beginning. He may have been attracted to me, but he was always fighting it. Fighting me. He wants me, but he wishes he didn't. And he's already made a decision. Rafe won't claim me, whatever that means.

I didn't know why before, but now I do. And I'm done.

I blink away the burning in my eyes. "Okay, well, this fragile human is out of here," I say, pulling out my phone.

"Adele—" He reaches for me, and I bat his hand away.

"Don't. Don't touch me, Rafe." My voice wobbles on

his name, and I force myself to meet his sorrowful gaze. "Please."

He holds his hands in the air. "Okay," he chokes, stepping back. "I won't touch you. Just let me get you home safely."

"No." I already have my phone out. "I'm calling a rideshare. We're done." I open up the app and request a car.

"I never meant to hurt you."

"Well, you did, but that's life." I shrug, lifting my chin, fighting back the tears. Saving them for when I'm away from here. When I'm alone.

I open the door to wait outside, but Rafe follows me out, still butt naked, except for the dish towel. "You wait inside," he coaxes. "I'll stay out." And with that, his motion blurs, and he drops to all fours, once more the beautiful, terrifying wolf.

I go back inside the house, but I don't take off my coat. Don't move past the foyer. I'm getting the hell out of Utah.

No wonder he was running hot and cold, pushing me away. He was keeping a secret from me. Many secrets. Do his friends know? Does his brother know?

What does claiming a mate even mean?

Who is Gabriel Dieter, and why did they hate each other?

I'm in a world where nothing makes sense. Where I don't belong.

Good thing I packed light. Technically, I brought nothing…

When my ride gets here, I have no idea where Rafe is. As if his wolf is lurking nearby, I dash from the front door to the car like I'm being chased. The poor driver looks at me like I'm insane. "Drive," I gasp. "Just drive."

With the glee of an amateur race car driver, she hits

the gas. We're halfway down the mountain when I spot him. A huge black wolf with orange tipped ears, sitting on a snowy hill. Adrenaline jolts through my body. I always imagined wolves as big, wild dogs, but nope, this thing is to a dog what a hatchback sedan is to a tank. Way bigger. Way more dangerous. The wolf's muzzle is closed, the fangs hidden, but it's lethalness is on display in every line of its big body.

That's Rafe. Impossible, but true. My heartbeat slows as if my body recognizes Rafe.

The wolf regards me, its posture regal, bright eyes fixing me to the spot. There's a flash of green as they catch the light.

He's beautiful. The orange tipped ears twitch forward, but the wolf is otherwise still. It doesn't look angry. It just looks... Sad.

Goosebumps run over my body as I put my hand to the glass. "Rafe," I mouth.

The wolf throws back his head and howls. The mournful sound follows me as the car swings around a corner, and the wolf that's Rafe drops out of sight.

10

Rafe

"Took you long enough," Deke says when I call him.

I'm not in the mood to explain why it took me so long to call. My wolf wouldn't let me change back into human right away, so I took him for a run. A sign I'm losing control. The moon madness, taking hold.

"Adele's fine. Got a last minute flight to Albuquerque. Sadie picked her up from the airport."

"Alone?"

"Sadie insisted. Said they needed a 'girl chat.' I thought it was a good idea. But I'm following them. You think I'd let Sadie out of my sight with all this shady shit Dieter's pulling?"

Once he says it, I hear the sounds of his big Mercedes' engine. My shoulders drift down an inch. "All right. Teddy's picking me up."

"You'll beat her to Taos, then. We've got some drive time. By the way, if my phone cuts out, it's because I'm in the canyon. What are your orders, Sarge?"

"We need to find out what the fuck Gabriel Dieter is up to."

"What happened?"

"Fucker shows up, toys with Adele, but doesn't hurt her. Then when I show up, he tells me he relinquishes his claim on her. That she's not his intended."

"What the fuck?"

"There's more. He had these weird eyes–almost like a snake's. I honestly don't know what kind of creature he could be, but he's powerful. He used an alpha command on me, and I felt it. I had to work to fight it."

"Fuck. So he's paranormal. You think he's a shifter? Or could he be a vampire?"

"No, he doesn't smell like a blood-sucker. I'll get the Tucson pack to check with the leech king, but I'm pretty sure Dieter's not one of them. He's some sort of shifter."

"Lion? Bear?"

"No. Something else. The question is, what?"

"We gotta find out. I don't know what his agenda is. He had Adele in his clutches. Then he said he was relinquishing her. He's toying with me."

"See, that's a clue. What shifter toys with their prey?"

"I'm not his prey."

"You're acting like it," Deke snaps back. "Never thought I'd see the day I had more sense than you, Sarge. You've got a mate. Claim her."

I feel like puking, remembering what it felt like to tell Adele I wasn't going to claim her. To know I'd hurt her. "I can't, Deke."

"Not claiming her will kill you."

"And being with me could kill her! I won't risk it."

"Bullshit. You can keep her safe. Just like Lance and I protect our mates."

"I'm the alpha. It's different for me."

Deke sighs. "Sarge, you're out of your damn mind."

ADELE

"Hey, there," Sadie says when I slide into her car at the Albuquerque airport. "You okay?"

"Yeah." I sink into the seat with a sigh. "I'm sorry I made you come all the way here to get me. I booked a last minute flight, and this airport was all I could get–"

"Shhh, it's okay." Sadie pats my knee before putting her hand back on the wheel.

I close my eyes, but I see Rafe the wolf watching me leave. *He looked so sad.*

Well, I'm sad, too. And he's the one who broke my heart.

"We have a lot to talk about." I swallow. I don't know how I'm going to explain about Rafe, Gabriel, the wolf–

"It's okay," Sadie says, as if she's reading my thoughts. "I know what's going on. All of it."

She does? My jaw works up and down before I finally can say, "You do?"

"Oh, yes." Sadie's mouth curls into a wry smile as she takes the Santa Fe relief route. "Did you ever wonder why Deke lives in a huge mountain lodge with all his military buddies? Deke was about as antisocial a guy as you can get, but he not only works with them, he lives with them."

"Well, yeah." She said it about her man, I didn't. "I figured he hates people, but he doesn't hate his military brothers as much as everyone else."

"There's that," Sadie says. "But there's also…" She raises a brow at me.

And it hits me. "Oh God. Oh my God." The band of brothers, the tight knit bond. Rafe couldn't keep the secret of what he is from Deke, would he? And if Rafe trusted Deke enough to tell him, maybe that means Deke isn't just in on the secret, he *shares* the secret…

"Yep." Sadie reads my thoughts once again.

I have to clarify. "Deke's….a…" I thought of this the whole plane ride from Utah but never suspected I'd be saying it out loud to one of my best friends. "A *werewolf?*"

"They prefer the term *wolf shifter* or just *shifter.* But yeah."

"Oh my God." What is my life right now?

"I know. It's a lot. I felt that way when I found out."

"You didn't tell anyone."

"I couldn't. No human can know."

"I got that," I say. "I won't tell anyone." No one would believe me if I did. They'd think I was going crazy.

Maybe I am going crazy. But if I am, Sadie's in the same boat. I can handle going out of my mind if I've got a friend along for the ride.

"Most of the time, if a human finds out the secret–that shifters exist–the shifter gets a vampire to mind wipe the human. Erase the memories."

A vampire?!

"—But you and me, we're the exception," Sadie continues. "We're special."

"No," I choke, Rafe's words echoing in my mind. "You might be special, but I'm not. He says I'm too fragile to be his mate. He's not claiming me. What does that even mean?"

"Oh, no." Sadie throws me a look that seems half-sympathetic, half-worried. "It means he's crazy." She checks her rearview mirror. She's been checking it a lot this drive. "Shifters can't be made, only born. So maybe it's biology or evolution or…anyway… in all the world, there's one person they connect to more than any other. Their true love. Their mate."

"Like soulmate?"

"Exactly, but it's ten thousand times more intense. All their shifter instincts kick in. It's more than love. You're the only one in the universe for them."

"And you have that with Deke." I can't help but smile.

"Yeah," Sadie says softly.

"I love that for you."

"Thanks. It's pretty great. We're gonna get married because it's a human convention, but in the pack's eyes, we're more than husband and wife." We drive a few more miles while I digest this. A little line appears on Sadie's forehead. "Rafe never told you any of this."

"Nope. I thought we got pretty close in Utah but not close enough, I guess."

"I'm sorry."

"Actually…I understand it. His parents were killed, and he had to look after Lance when he was just fifteen. All his control issues are around trying to keep the people he loves safe. So I guess he doesn't think he can add one more to that list. Especially because I'm human and *fragile*." I make air quotes with my fingers around the word "fragile."

"Yeah, Deke told me Rafe never wanted any of them to get mates. Not just because we're human. Even if we were wolf shifters, he was against it. He thinks we weaken the pack."

Despite myself, I flinch. "Ouch."

"You see, shifters have these amazing healing proper-ties. Charlie said Lance had all these bullet holes in him after one of their missions, and then he just healed up in a day or two."

My eyes inexplicably fill with tears. Every piece of information I learn about Rafe's kind makes the gulf between us even bigger. Makes me miss him even more. Wish that things could be different. I want what Sadie and Deke have. And Charlie and Lance.

"So to them, humans seem super vulnerable," Sadie goes on. "So I get it. We're the weak link, especially because we're human. But Deke doesn't see me as a weakness. Mates make a pack stronger. But I guess, in Rafe's eyes, it's more people to protect."

Her words hit me like a bowling ball to the chest. "I wish he wasn't such a control freak."

"Yep. It's an alpha thing. You have it too," Sadie says in her gentle way. Only Sadie can deliver a verbal punch to the gut so sweetly. "That's why you try to take care of all of us."

"I'm not like Rafe," I grumble. "He's hot and cold. It's crazy!" Of course, I ran hot and cold too. I couldn't deal with my attraction to him, and I blamed it on the fact we were boss and employee. And then I got naked in an outdoor pool and seduced him. I groan, covering my face with my hand. "This is a mess."

"It is," Sadie says. "And Rafe has been infuriating. He's tearing himself apart, trying to figure out what to do. The wolf side of him probably wants to claim you ASAP, but he's trying to do what's best for you and his pack."

"No, he made up his mind. Did Deke tell you about what happened with this guy Gabriel Dieter?"

Sadie bites her lip for a mile and a half, glancing in the rearview mirror again. "Deke hasn't told me much about him, so I think he's connected to a top secret mission. All I know is Dieter's dangerous. And I guess he was messing with you because he knew it would mess with Rafe."

"He didn't hurt me. It was all very weird." I shiver. "I don't know why I spent as much time with him as I did. It's like my normal instincts were suppressed. I even saw one of Dieter's employees–the guy was in a serious amount of military gear. Red flags all over the place, but I just didn't pick up on them."

"Don't beat yourself up. Dieter is rich and has tons of connections. He's probably used to getting what he wants. If he wanted to meet and spend time with you, he'd engineer the perfect moment." She glances in the rearview mirror.

I crane my neck. There's a familiar black Mercedes G63 following us. "That's Deke, isn't it?" I say in a resigned tone.

"Yeah. He's worried about us. Because Dieter. Plus he's super protective—"

"Because of the mate thing." Once more, I have to fight back tears.

Sadie turns onto the road that leads to my neighborhood and adds, "The full moon can affect things too."

"Oh my God, it's a full moon," I say. "Maybe that's why they invented the word 'lunatic.' It was really a bunch of wolf shifters." A hysterical laugh bubbles up in my gut and spills over. "It's like a bunch of women cycling together, except it's a bunch of wolf shifters on the same cycle." I bend in half, breathless with laughter. Sadie watches, looking sympathetic.

I laugh harder. I'm still howling when Sadie pulls into my driveway, and Charlie comes out of my house and down the path to greet us. She opens my door, takes one look at me rocking in the seat, whimpered giggles escaping me while tears track down my cheeks, and raises a brow.

"I see she's taking this well," Charlie says to Sadie.

"Let's go inside," Sadie says.

"Sounds good." Charlie takes my hand to guide me out of the car. "I didn't call Tabitha because she doesn't

155

know… you know. And I didn't know if you wanted to talk that out some more."

Sadie waves to Deke, who parks in front of my house. Standing guard, I guess. Sadie told me the cartel threat is gone, but Deke is known for being overprotective.

Both of my friends help me inside, but once I'm there instinct takes over. I head to the kitchen and put on an apron. Preheat the oven and pull out a baking sheet, then grab a container out of the freezer. I have profiterole dough saved for just this moment.

"What's she doing?" Charlie whispers to Sadie.

"Stress baking." Sadie waves Charlie to a stool. "C'mon. It'll be a while before dessert's ready, but it'll be worth it."

"Mmmm, sugar. Just what this baby mama needs." Charlie angles herself awkwardly on the stool. She's not showing yet, but she rests her hand on her pregnant belly.

The whisk I was holding clatters to the floor. "Oh my God," I choke. "Charlie. You're—"

"Pregnant with a puppy?" She winks.

Oh my God. Sadie told me Lance was a shifter, but I didn't put it together until now. *My friend is pregnant with a shifter's baby.*

"Is that what they call it?" My voice is shrill. My hands flutter to my own belly. Rafe and I had sex a million times. What if my birth control failed?

"Relax, Adele," Charlie says quickly, straightening. "I'm not going to give birth to a puppy."

Sadie frowns at her. "No more jokes. She's processing a lot." She hops off her stool, grabs the whisk and cleans up, offering me a glass of water and rubbing my back while I drink it.

"How are you doing?" I ask Charlie, when I can speak again. "I would be out of my mind right now."

"I have a lot of help." She pats her stomach. "There are other humans who have mated with shifters."

Mated. There's that word again.

"I want this baby. I love Lance. I resisted him because he was a player, but you know what wolf shifters never do with their mates? Cheat or leave."

"It's a perk," Sadie nods.

Another rush of tears. This time I let them fall. I pause in beating the shit outta of the creme patisserie. "He said I was a distraction."

"He did what?" Charlie and Sadie flank me, both giving me side hugs.

I wave a whisk. It flings custard everywhere, leaving egg yolk-yellow drips on my wood cabinets, but that's okay. After a bout of stress baking comes a bout of stress cleaning. "It was in the heat of the moment. I'm trying not to hold it against him, but my mémère said to believe what people tell you, even when they're drunk or their emotions are high. Especially then. Their filters are gone, so they're telling the truth." I swallow. "He sees me as a distraction, guys. I'm not a central figure in his life."

"No," both my friends gasp. "That's not it at all–" Sadie says at the same time Charlie adds, "You're his mate. You are *the* central figure in his life."

I hold up a hand. "He's not claiming me."

Charlie and Sadie look stricken, but they don't contradict me. I point a whisk at them. "We had some good moments together. But it's over."

11

Rafe

Since I got home last night, I've been attempting to drink myself into a stupor, which unfortunately is impossible for a shifter. The numbness only lasts ten minutes, tops, before my body processes the alcohol. Still, it's worth the effort even for the momentary relief.

Adele is gone. I drove her away, and I deserve all the pain blasting through my chest right now.

But I did the right thing.

I did.

Adele's association with me nearly got her tangled in Dieter's dark plans, whatever they may have been. I still don't know why he thought she was his mate nor what made him change his mind. I don't understand what he knows about my parents' death.

I try to keep my thoughts focused on him, try to put the pieces of the puzzle together, but they keep swinging back to Adele.

To the sound of her voice breaking. The hurt on her face.

Fates, I'm almost hoping for moon madness to come and take me now. At least it would be better than living like this.

I open the fridge door and stare blankly at the contents. Looks like Channing went to the Grille and stocked up on takeout boxes. I've stood here and stared a dozen times, as if I can conjure up something Adele's cooked. I'd eat a vegan meal if I knew she made it. I'd even eat another sprig of parsley.

Channing, Lance and Deke come in all together, like they planned an intervention or something. I guess I don't blame them. None of them would survive a confrontation with me alone right now.

"How are you doing, Sarge?" Channing doesn't make eye contact.

I don't bother answering. I just stand inside the open refrigerator door, hoping it might teleport me to some other existence. One where I can have Adele and keep her safe.

"Any word on Dieter?" I demand.

"He's in the wind," Lance reports. "He's left Utah but no telling where he is now. Fucker has houses all over the world."

I try to get my shit together. To act like the alpha I'm supposed to be. "I think he's going to make his move soon," I hear myself say, but it's an out of body experience. Like I'm standing back watching myself say the words. "He let Adele go–which tells us he no longer believes she's his mate."

"Yeah because what sort of shifter would let their mate go?" Channing asks, then winces.

I let her go.

Fuck. I did. I was an idiot.

"Would you please explain to me why Adele is not

here, as your claimed mate, under this roof where we can protect her at all times?" Lance demands. "Because the way I see it, you left her hanging in the wind back there, and it makes no fucking sense to me."

A yawning horror threatens to engulf me.

My mate requires my protection, and I abandoned her. My need to have my loved ones safe made me blind to the most obvious truth—she isn't safer apart from me. There's no disassociating myself from her—not when she's my fated mate. No one can change fate. Not even a controlling asshole like me.

"I've got to go," I say, shoving my hand in my pocket for my keys.

"Where are you going?" Lance calls after me.

"To claim my mate," I shout over my shoulder. "If I can make her forgive me."

ADELE

Step one to getting over Rafe: find a new job. And it turns out it's the easiest thing on my list to check off because when I check my charged phone, a message is waiting for me. I don't recognize the number, but it's a Taos area code. The man speaking has a British accent.

"Good day, Madame Fabre. I am Mr. Button and I'm calling to inform you of a private chef position that's just opened up in my household. We haven't advertised, but we received a reference saying we must hire you. If you are available today, I'd like to interview you at the following address…"

I hit redial before the message finishes and confirm the appointment to Mr. Button's voicemail. "It just so happens I'm free today."

Finally, something is going my way. I dress and get dolled up quickly. No amount of makeup can hide the fact that after my friends went home, I was up all night crying, but I do my best.

The address is easy to find, and I know the job's legit because the home is a mansion set on several acres, near Julia Roberts' Taos home.

"Right this way, madame," the man says with a crisp British accent. He's dressed in a suit with coattails, answering the door in the middle of the day. Either he's a butler or Downtown Abbey is filming in this house.

I follow him through the house, marveling at the giant gilt framed works of art and oriental rugs covering the floor. This place is bigger than the Park City mansion and decorated like a museum. It screams old money. Another good sign.

The butler leads me to a study of sorts, with a heavy wooden bookshelf full of bound books reaching the ceiling on one side, and a wall of windows overlooking a several story drop into a ravine on the other.

"Please, make yourself at home." The butler gestures to one of several leather bound chairs in front of a desk. "The master will be with you soon. Shall I bring you some tea?"

"Please." I smooth the front of my dress. "Although I do have a few questions about the job."

"The master can answer them all," the butler says with an air of finality.

"One thing," I say before he can exit. "The family I'll be working for, are they the Buttons?"

"Oh no, ma'am, that's my surname. Your employer will be Mr. Gabriel Dieter."

The door closes behind him with a thud as I gasp. Oh no.

Gabriel Dieter–again?

What is going on?

Whatever it is, I don't want to be in the middle of it.

I stride to the door and try the handle.

It's locked.

"Hey!" I shout, slamming my fist against the polished wood. The door is so old and heavy, I wouldn't be surprised if my shrieks are muffled. The only one who's going to hear is the butler, and he just locked me in.

There might not be anyone else in the house, either.

I can't believe I fucking fell for this again. Fuck Gabriel Dieter.

I race to the window. I can throw a chair through it, but then I'll be jumping out of the second story of a mansion. Plus, this room overlooks a ravine. Beautiful, but those sage brush and rocks at the bottom will break me before they break my fall.

My hand's on my cell phone. *Please get service.* There's a blinking telling me it's roaming, but a call will go through. But who to call? 911? What do I say? "Help, I came to a job offer in a mansion like an idiot, and now I'm trapped?"

If this was a normal situation, I'd call Tabitha and Charlie to get me out. They'd bust down the door. Charlie would show her US Postal service ID like a "get out of jail free" card. Once the door was open, Tabitha would unleash the whirlwind she is. Sadie's too sweet for confrontation, but she'd drive the getaway car.

But if this is Dieter, something more is at stake here. And I can't involve my friends in something dangerous. There's only one person I can call. The man who I can trust. Who's always had my back.

Rafe.

Rafe

I pull up at Adele's house, but her truck isn't there.

My phone buzzes. *Adele.*

I hit the answer button so hard I nearly break it.

"Oh my God, Rafe. Thank God you answered." Her voice is thready with a panicked edge.

I whirl from the fridge, instantly alert. "Baby, where are you?"

"At this house." She rattles off an address. "I thought it was a job offer. It seemed too good to be true. And—" She gasps, out of breath.

"Slow down, princess, talk to me."

"They locked me in. I can't get out. The windows are too high up. Rafe, the guy said it's Gabriel Dieter's house, and now I'm locked in."

I'm already out the door, car keys in hand. "Hang on, Adele. Sit tight, stay calm."

"Rafe, I need you."

"I'm already coming baby, sit tight. Hold fast."

Fifteen minutes later, Channing's traced Adele's call to the location. Deke's driving, Lance is on the line. I'm holding both Deke's phone and mine—I kept the call with Adele going, but I'm muted, so I can bark orders without scaring her. I can still hear Adele's frantic breathing.

"I've got Kylie monitoring dark web channels," Lance's voice crackles through Deke's burner phone. "She's mobilized the Tucson packs. They're flying in as back up. Colonel Johnson's coming too, to direct the boots on the ground."

"They don't have to do that—"

"For all we know, Dieter's brought an army. We're not fucking around. Adele's family. We'll all fight to get her back."

My throat has closed. I can't speak.

Lance hears my silence and gets it. His voice softens, "Kylie says to pass on this message to you: "Rafe, we're in this together. You don't have to go alone.""

"Thank you, brother," I say finally.

"Anytime. Go get your mate."

I switch phones and unmute myself on mine. "Adele?"

"I'm here." She sounds calmer.

"We've got your location. Stay safe. We'll be there soon."

"Thank you."

Deke mutters a curse as he takes a tight curve and gravel sprays from under the tires.

"Rafe?" Adele's voice rises.

"It's okay, princess." I keep my voice calm. "Have you seen Dieter?"

"No. The butler said he was going to come, right before he locked me in."

Cold fire burns in my veins. I calm my wolf, so I keep a clear head.

Adele is saying, "I don't understand. What does Dieter want with me?"

"I don't know," I answer honestly. "But it doesn't matter. You're safe, and we're going to get you out."

"Okay."

"Stay on the line. If our call drops, it's okay. We've got your location, and we're coming for you."

I mute her just in time–Deke screeches to a halt in front of huge ornate gates. He reverses his G63, backs up a few yards and guns the Mercedes forward. I grip the oh-shit handle a second before we smash into the iron. The gates are more than decorative, but they give way with an agonizing screech.

"German engineering." Deke's got a crazed grin on his face. He loves the psycho shit. "I'm telling you."

The Mercedes roars forward, hurtling down the private lane towards a sprawling Tudor home. The front fender's bent up, but the wheels still work.

"Hold up," I raise a hand as we get closer. Between us and the house there's a fancy fountain surrounded by decorative shrubs. The landscaping is completely out of place for the high mesa, but it wouldn't be the first time a wealthy family drained their well putting a British style garden in an arid area.

Beyond the ridiculous landscaping are rows and rows of soldiers in full military gear. Flak vests, helmets. Bukly AK-47s that I bet have been modified to shoot silver bullets.

Dieter's army.

"I see them," Deke says. He angles the Mercedes across the road, so we could take cover behind it.

I lift my burner phone. "Channing?"

"Here, Sarge. I picked up Lance. We're right behind you." I hear the roar of the humvee coming up the private road behind us.

"We've got trouble," I bark. "A whole platoon of Dieter's private army. Just like Switzerland."

"Shit," Lance swears. Channing must have me on speaker. "How are we going to pull this off?"

"Adele's in a room at the back of the house, overlooking the ravine. We could make a distraction and someone sneaks in the back." They'd have to repel down with Adele strapped to them. Not ideal.

"We've got air support coming," Channing adds. "Teddy's on his way, and he's got his brothers with them."

"Shit, we better wrap things up before then." Seven angry werebears in warbirds is the last thing this sensitive situation needs.

I peer out the window at Dieter's private army. They

haven't moved, haven't spoken. They look like fucking Storm Troopers. Creepy.

"I got Jackson on the phone," Lance says. "He says he can get a few tanks over there."

"Fucking awesome," Deke mutters. "I've got grenades." He's got crazy wolf eyes again—the look he wore 24/7 before he met Sadie.

"No, no," I rub my face. "We can't go to war, not like this. This is civilian territory. Besides, Adele's in there. We can't ram through the troops and risk compromising the structural integrity of the house."

"Rafe?" Adele's soft voice cuts through everything. I unmute the phone and put it to my ear.

"I'm here, Adele. We're out front. We just gotta get to you. Dieter's got his men out front."

"Be safe," she begs.

"We will. I promise."

There's movement by the front door. An unhelmeted man marches down the center of the platoon. A commanding officer, I'd bet my life on it. He holds something up. A grenade? A device?

"Sargeant Lightfoot," he shouts. "Master Dieter wishes to speak to you." The man has a thick Germanic accent. He probably shot at me in Switzerland when we tried to spy on Dieter's private eagle's nest.

I glare at him but he makes no other move. He waits patiently, holding the device aloft. A cell phone. "Phone call for you," he says.

"Hang on." I mutter, and open the passenger side door and get out slowly.

"Sarge," Deke warns.

"I got this."

"Rafe, no," Lance says. "It's a ploy—"

"I know. Dieter's playing games. But maybe I can

bargain with him." Adele for me. I pocket my phone and wink at Deke. "Once Adele's safe, you can hit the house with all the fire power you got. Light it up. I'll survive."

Deke shakes his head, but he lets me exit the car. I walk slowly, my hands spread at my sides to show I'm unarmed.

The lieutenant stands still, holding the phone and nothing else. No weapons. Not that he needs a weapon. His men are bristling with them. But none raise their guns as I approach. A good sign.

When I'm face to face with the commanding officer, the phone crackles to life.

"Hello, Mr. Lightfoot," Dieter says in a pleasant tone. "So nice of you to visit."

I shake my head. "You're not even here, are you?"

"Alas, I have other business."

"You have Adele. Let her go."

"I thought we had a deal. Your mate in trade for the information you seek for your revenge."

"I made no such deal. Give me Adele."

"Why? What does the life of one human matter…"

"She's my mate." My roar echoes around the yard. "Mine. I don't care how many men I have to mow down, I'm getting her back."

"What about your revenge?"

"What kind of sick game are you playing here?"

ADELE

I'm crouched in the library, holding my phone to my ear. Holding my breath.

Rafe has me on the line, and he didn't put me back on mute. I can hear everything clearly.

"She's my mate," he growls again.

Warmth spreads through me.

A slow, creepy chuckle comes from Dieter. "So you choose her over your revenge?"

"I choose her over everything on this planet. You can take your information and shove it up your–"

"Understood. Very well. My men have orders to stand down."

"What the fuck?" Rafe snaps, but then there's a pause. "No tricks?" he adds warily.

"No tricks. You made your choice. Go and get your mate."

And then there's just a growl, followed by the sound of Rafe's even breathing.

I stand. "Rafe," I call. I hear him through the phone, running, his boots crunching over the gravel. Another growl and a grunt.

"I'm in," he calls, and I hear his voice through the phone and very faintly through the door. "Adele!"

"Rafe," I shout, banging on the door for good measure. "Back here! Follow the hall to the very back!"

His boots pound over the hardwood floors. I grab the locked doorknob and twist it, trying to rattle it, even though it's locked and holds fast.

"Adele!" Rafe's voice sounds on the other side of the door.

"It's locked," I shout.

"Back up, baby," he orders.

I scramble backwards and duck behind a chair for good measure.

A roar and a thud. The room shudders. Another roar, a thud. Books fall off the shelves. I cover my head, but can't help peeking out. The room shakes. A few more thuds, and the door is toast.

A hand rips through the wood. Splinters go flying.

Then Rafe surges through the broken wreckage of the door.

"Adele!"

"Rafe." I rise on wobbly legs, and he scoops me up. I hang on, my head against his shoulder as he carries me like a bride back through Dieter's house and out into the winter air.

ADELE

"You can put me down now," I insist as Rafe carries me across the threshold of his lodge. He hasn't let me go since we left Dieter's. We rode in the backseat of Deke's Mercedes—which looks like it's been off-roading and fallen fender first off a mountain.

"Nope," he grunts. "No can do, princess. I'm never letting you go."

I blink at him. "What does that mean?"

He knows what I'm asking. "It means I was an idiot. The biggest idiot who ever walked this Earth. I thought I could keep you safer by staying away, but all I did was break both our hearts and get you kidnapped again."

I furrow my brow. "Was I kidnapped? I still don't understand what that was all about. What did Dieter want?"

"I don't know, but I will never let him near you again. I promise."

Rafe carries me into his bedroom and kicks the door shut. My entire body tingles with awareness. Excitement. Now that I know what Rafe is, I feel like a virgin about to have sex for the first time.

With a wolf.

"Are you claiming me, Rafe?"

His eyes flash green. "Damn straight." He dives onto the bed with me still in his arms, and we both bounce and fall into each other. "I mean, if you'll have me."

"Yes." I've never been more sure of anything in my life. "You're mine."

I'm rewarded with Rafe's boyish smile–the one that makes him look ten years younger, the weight of the world erased from his face. "I am definitely yours. And you're mine."

"Are you going to be a bossy pain in my butt?" I ask.

He flips me to my back and pins my wrists beside my head. "You know it." He nuzzles into my neck and nips the skin there.

"Aren't you afraid I'm too fragile?" I can't help but bring it up. I'm still hurt over it.

He winces. "You're not too fragile. You're the strongest human I know, Adele. The only thing that's fragile is this." He taps his chest in the place over his heart. "You've already captured it, so try not to crush me."

"I won't crush you. I think you're crushing me, though." I pretend to resist the hold he has on my wrists. The bulge of his cock presses in the notch between my legs. I roll my hips to meet his.

He lifts off me enough to tug my coat off my arms then my blouse. I'm wearing a plum satin bra, which makes him growl in approval.

"Does this mean you won't get crazy over-protective?"

He trails kisses down my belly then unzips the side zipper of my skirt. "No chance of that, princess. You will have to surrender to my bossy protection or suffer the consequences."

I work the button on his jeans. "What consequences are those?"

His smile grows feral. "I think you might remember

171

from before..." He rolls me to my belly and pulls my skirt off my hips. "Mmm, matching panties. Almost too beautiful to take off." He pulls them down. "But I have your punishment to consider."

I part my legs and lift my ass. "Am I in trouble?"

His hand claps down on my cheek, stinging me. He immediately massages away the shock of it. "Big trouble, Adele." Another slap, this time on the other cheek. When he rubs, his hand feels gloriously warm. He picks my hips up, pulling me onto my knees, my chest still pressed into the bedding, my ass presented to him.

"When you disobey, there will be consequences."

"Mmm." I give my hips a little shimmy.

Rafe chuckles and starts spanking me in earnest, laying a half dozen quick slaps down before he stops and rubs again.

It smarts, but it feels good, too. For as much as I resisted Rafe's dominance outside of the bedroom, I love it here. It's exactly what I craved most but never knew I needed.

"I need to know you're safe, Adele. I'm in a dangerous business, and you're the most important thing in the world to me." He delivers three more swift spanks.

Tears pop into my eyes, but it's not from the spanking —it's because of his words.

"I'll let you protect me, Rafe," I promise.

"Of course, you did call me today, so that deserves a reward." He pushes me back to my belly, leans over and nips my ear. "Was it hard to ask for help, Adele?" His voice is rich and seductive. Gloriously rough and smooth at the same time.

"No." It's the truth. Whatever my hang ups with asking for help are, they don't apply to Rafe anymore. I've let him in. "I knew you'd come. I wanted you to rescue me."

Rafe surges behind me, grinding the bulge of his cock into the cleft of my ass at the same time his teeth graze my shoulder. "Fates, Adele, I almost marked you. Hearing that... it's what a male wolf needs."

I twist to see him, and he rolls me back on my back. "What else does a male wolf need?" I purr.

"I have to mark you." He says it like it's a bad thing, but I'm not afraid. Sadie and Charlie already explained it to me. It's how he claims me—how he permanently embeds his scent into me, so every other wolf will know I'm taken.

"I can't wait," I tell him, pulling his Henley up to expose his ripped abs.

He grins and whips the shirt off over his head. "First I have to taste you." He crawls backward, pulling my panties the rest of the way off my legs as I unhook my bra. When he sees it unclasped, he snatches the front of it and pulls it off my arms, sending it arcing through the air to the floor in the corner.

His nostrils flare and eyes glow green as he simply stares down at my naked body.

"Rafe," I encourage, reaching for him.

He lowers his head and sucks my dark nipple into his mouth. I feel the electric pulsing heat zing from my nipple straight to my core. I roll my hips beneath his, searching for something more.

"Why are your jeans still on?" I pant.

"Hush. You're not in charge, princess." Rafe crawls lower and hooks his hands beneath my knees pushing them up wide. He licks into me, his tongue parting my nether lips and swirling around the inside. I jerk at the pleasure of it. My belly shudders in and out, my inner thighs tighten and tremble, but he holds them firmly open. I lift my core to meet his mouth, and he sucks everywhere, licking, nipping, driving me wild.

"Rafe," I moan.

"That's right, princess. Rafe's here to help."

"Oh Jesus," I chant, my mind slipping out of my ears as he drives me to a frenzy with that clever tongue of his. "More. Oh God, Rafe." He finds my clit and flicks it with his tongue at the same time he screws one finger inside me. "Rafe."

He screws a second finger in and uses the tips to stroke my inner wall.

I cry out, the shock of pleasure almost too much to receive, but he's relentless, stroking my G-spot, sucking my clit. I moan loudly, forgetting he lives in a compound with others. I can't hold it in. The pressure building up is driving me crazy. "Oh God!" I come, bucking out my release against his mouth and fingers. He changes the motion of his fingers to a fast pump, fucking me with them as I ride his mouth with spasmodic undulations of my hips.

"Oh my God. Holy… wow. Just wow," I pant, unable to shut up. I'm both wrung out and still greedy.

"Did you like your reward, Adele?" Rafe's eyes are completely wolf-like. He's magnificent.

"Claim me," I beg.

He flips me to my belly and shucks his pants and boxer briefs. "I'll be careful," he promises.

"I know you will." I trust him. This is a guy who worries about me slipping on ice. He's not going to hurt me.

He climbs up behind me and rubs the head of his cock at my entrance. I'm already wet and swollen, ready to receive him. One push and he's in. We both groan our pleasure.

"Adele, you feel so good," he rasps behind me.

I lift my hips to take him deeper. He strokes in and out

of me, and nothing has ever felt more right. More fulfilling. My eyes roll back in my head with the perfection of it.

We fall silent, nothing but the rasp of our quickened breaths, the slap of skin on skin, the rustle of bedsheets. I brace my hands against the headboard to keep from sliding up.

"Adele," Rafe rasps. I hear the mounting desperation in his tone. Feel it in the urgency of his thrusts.

"I love you, Rafe." I don't know why I picked that moment to tell him, but he goes wild behind me, thrusting in so hard the bed slams against the wall. Our bodies bounce on the bed.

"Adele... *Adele!*"

It's too rough, but I wouldn't stop him for the world, especially when I hear him roar his release. He thrusts into me, dropping down to cover my body with his, squeezing me tight in an embrace. His teeth graze my shoulder, then puncture the skin. I jerk and stiffen at the pain, but he immediately releases me.

"Oh Fates, are you okay? Adele, tell me you're okay. I'm so sorry." My body's already relaxed, drugged by endorphins, or maybe by the serum he released into my skin. He licks the place he bit me.

"It's perfect. I'm great. I love you," I reassure him.

He pulls out, rolls me to my back, and claims my mouth. "I love you so much, Adele." He drops kisses all over my face. "Not just wolf love. Crazy fucking human love, too. I can't live without you."

I laugh at his frenzy of affection, receiving it all. "I love you, Rafe. I love you, I love you, I love you."

"I'm sorry, I sort of lost control there at the end. Are you okay? Did I hurt you?"

I laugh. "It was amazing."

He settles in the cradle of my legs. "Well, there's more

where that came from, princess." And unbelievably, I find he's hard already, his cock prodding my entrance. I wrap my legs around his back and hook my ankles, pulling him against me, so he sinks into me.

I'm sore, but I want more. Everything Rafe has to offer, I want to receive.

~

Rafe

I make Adele come three more times before I hear her stomach rumble and realize it's long past dinner time.

"You're hungry," I groan, pissed at myself for not seeing to my mate's needs. I climb off the bed and get a washcloth to clean her.

"I'll bet you are, too. Now I know why you were such a pain in my ass over the meat thing. Wolves are definitely carnivores."

I stroke between her legs with the warm washcloth, even though I'd rather leave her covered in my cum. She's marked forever now, though. No need to stake my claim again.

"No, I was a pain in the ass because being around you drove my wolf wild, and I was pissed that I didn't think I could have you. I would give anything to have a do-over and sit and eat your red beans and win your affection with my praise, like Channing did."

"Channing," she says with a laugh. "You were actually jealous of Channing, weren't you?"

"Don't even talk about it," I warn. I'm not still threatened, not really, but the memory still chafes.

"Come on. Isn't he, like, barely over twenty?"

"Women find him attractive."

Adele laughs and climbs off the bed, wrapping her

arms around my waist and pressing her soft body against mine. "You're being ridiculous. You know that, right?"

"Yes," I grumble. "I do know." I wrap my hand around the back of her head to lift her face to mine. I stroke her soft brown skin with my thumb. "Forgive me. Not having you made me crazy."

She lifts on her toes and gives me a soft kiss. The kind that starts with her lips moving against mine, then deepens into something more. My tongue sweeps between her lips, my hand drops to her ass and squeezes.

I hear her stomach rumble again. "Sorry!" I spring back. "I'm sorry, you're hungry. I just can't get enough of you."

"Let's go see if I can find you some meat," she says with a laugh, pulling one of my t-shirts out of a drawer and putting it on.

"Um, not like that."

She rolls her eyes.

"Have you seen your legs, princess? You slay with those legs. Here, put these on." I toss her a pair of my sweats, which she tugs on and rolls down several times at the waist.

"Not really my style, but I'll make an exception for you."

I swat her ass as she sashays past me and down the stairs to the kitchen, where she starts her magic.

Twenty minutes later, she's made a full meal out of left-over pork she found in the freezer from the pig roast. She uncorks a bottle of white wine and pours us both a glass. I dig out emergency candles and light them, arranging them in the middle of the table.

The guys must not be around, or the scent of the food would have brought them running. Maybe they gave us space for her claiming.

We sit down at the table, just the two of us. She lifts her

glass of wine. Her skin glows in the candlelight, her gaze is only for me, her smile warm and inviting.

Mine. My wolf is smug.

"To us," Adele says.

I clink her glass with mine. "To you, Adele. You're my everything."

12

Adele

Taos is so festive during the holiday season. I hadn't appreciated the decorations as much in the past weeks, but now walking past the plaza, holding Rafe's hand, I appreciate the Christmas Card-worthy beauty of my town more and more.

"So what are we doing here?" I ask him. "Don't tell me that you need to go last minute Christmas shopping."

"Nope, already made 'em. Everyone's getting their very own trash can art sculpture."

I roll my eyes and Rafe chuckles. He's been doing that more–laughing and smiling. The other night Channing made a dumb joke, and Rafe didn't even glare at him.

"Well what are we doing here? I've got to get back to the house." I'm prepping for tomorrow, when I'll be cooking Christmas dinner for everyone at the lodge. It'll be all of us except for Tabitha, who left to go antiquing the same day Dieter kidnapped me. We're hoping to video chat with her later.

"I'm giving you your gift."

"But it's not yet Christmas," I protest, even though the pack's celebrating Christmas four days early so Lance and Charlie can head to her parents.

I whirl to face him, but my boots hit a patch of ice. I go flying, only to end up in a dramatic tango pose in Rafe arms.

"Got you." He kisses my forehead.

"My high heeled boots strike again," I mutter.

"You wear those boots all you want, princess," he murmurs as he sets me carefully back on my feet. "I'll be at your side to catch you if you fall."

Little does he know that's why I wore these boots in the first place.

"This way." He takes my hand and leads me across the street to a side lane that's for pedestrians only.

"Oh no." I tug on his hand. "I don't want to go that way." It'll take me right past The Chocolatier. I can't bear to see my shop closed up, windows dark during the holiday shopping rush.

"Adele," he says gently, swinging me to face him and cupping my cheeks in his rough hands. "Do you trust me?"

I swallow. "Yes."

But I hold my breath as we head up the alley. I could close my eyes, but I'm already leaning on Rafe's arm. When he tugs me to face the shop, my trepidation turns to wonder.

My little shop is glowing, lights from within spilling over the banks of snow. The path to the front stoop is shoveled, and the landlord's notice is down from the door. The windows are polished and gleaming. It looks ready to accept customers, even though there's no one inside

"What is this?" I swallow because if the landlord already got someone new in the building, I'm not ready to face it.

"This is your Christmas present," Rafe says.

I furrow my brow. "What do you mean?"

"The Chocolatier is ready for business. The guys all pitched in and brought over your stuff from the landlord's storage. Sadie and Charlie told me where everything needed to go, and they helped clean up."

"But, what about the landlord? The back rent?"

"All clear."

"Rafe, did you pay it?"

"Didn't have to. I talked to the landlord. You'll find I can be very persuasive."

My knees wobble, and he catches my hips, steadying me. "Merry Christmas, princess."

"Rafe, it's too much." I don't care what he's saying, there's no way my landlord forgave all that back rent. Rafe must've paid something, and if he did, I'm going to be beholden to him.

"Adele, you work hard. I could watch you work all hours to gain back what your biz partner stole from you, or I could make it right. And I don't want you working all hours. Less time for me." He shrugs. "And I want all the time with you I can get."

"It's too much." I shake my head.

"Not even a fraction of what you've given me. So, princess, are you going to accept my gift?"

I bite my lip. Mémère would be the first to tell me I don't need a man to be successful, but if she met Rafe, she would approve of him right away. "You've got yourself a good one," she'd tell me and wink.

"I'll pay you back," I say.

Rafe presses a finger to my lips. "We'll work it out," he says. He presents me with a shiny gold key. "New locks on every door." He dangles it in front of me, and I slowly hold out a hand.

"I'll take it on one condition. You've got to tell me what you told the landlord to get him to let me open up again."

He shakes his head with a sigh, but his cheek curves. "Fine. I bought the building."

"What?" I shriek so loud, snow falls from one of the lamp posts. "Oh my God. Rafe, I can't believe you."

"No?" He shrugs. "I'd do anything for you."

I throw myself at him. At the last second, my boots skid, but it doesn't matter because Rafe catches me.

He'll always catch me.

The snow starts falling as we share a rom com movie worthy kiss. It's the darkest day of the year, but the darkness makes the stars shine brighter. They twinkle like my mémère's diamonds, and I know she's smiling down on me.

Rafe

Christmas Day never meant much to me. Shifters don't really celebrate it, except to fit in with humans. After our parents were gone, we didn't celebrate anything. There was no reason, plus I was too busy keeping Lance and myself safe and alive.

Adele brings all that to me. The joy. The light.

And I know we're going to have some good arguments when she realizes I'm not going to charge her rent. And another argument when she finds out how many of her dark chocolate caramels Channing consumed when he was moving her stuff. You'd think that werewolves would be allergic to chocolate but not him.

"Has anyone heard from Tabitha?" Charlie asks, walking in from the kitchen with a pile of cookies for the coffee table. She sets them down and shakes her phone. "I keep trying to get her on the phone, but it's going straight to voicemail."

"She said she's driving through a bunch of dead zones, right?" Sadie pipes up.

"Yeah, but we set up a time to video chat since she couldn't be here with us." Charlie shrugs and climbs over the tattered piles of wrapping paper to sit in Lance's lap.

I survey the living room. The whole pack and our mates are here. I never thought my wolf would feel so satisfied, seeing us all gathered in one place, but he is.

The only one missing: my mate. She's in the kitchen, stirring a pot of gumbo.

Channing got everyone moose themed things. Some sort of joke. Which is why Adele's wearing an apron that reads *Merry Christmoose*.

"I can't believe you're actually wearing that thing," I mutter. My wolf would be annoyed that Adele's wearing the gift from another member of my pack, but since I've claimed her, he's calmed down a ton.

"What? I like it." She turns her back on me and sticks a wooden spoon into a bubbling pot. She blows on the red sauce to cool it and tastes it. "Needs sugar." She starts to slip away to grab it, and I pull her close.

I touch the side of my mouth. "You've got a little sauce on you."

"Do I really?" She wrinkles her nose at me.

"No," I say and kiss her.

"Mmm." She wriggles in my arms. "I'm still mad at you," she whispers against my lips.

"Oh?"

"If you bought the building that means you're my landlord. I thought we were done with the whole boss/employee power struggle shit."

"Do you want to be done with it? Because I'll sign the

papers to give you the building right here, right now." I gesture in the direction of my office.

Her eyes go wide.

"Or…" I slide a hand across her waist, turning her so she's facing the sink, and I'm pressed against her back. "We could keep playing the game." I slip my hand below the waistband of her skirt, and my fingers find satin and lace. "Our quarterly inspections could get real interesting."

"Rafe, not here," she complains, but her voice is breathless. A few light touches, and her slickness drenches my fingers.

"In my office," I command, like she's an employee about to get a reprimand. I withdraw my fingers and smirk.

She turns the burner down, tosses her dark hair and flounces past me, playing along.

There's a definite swagger to my walk as I follow. I lock the door behind me, then swipe my forearm across the desk to clear it of all contents.

"Rafe!" Adele catches my laptop before it clatters to the floor. "You're crazy."

"Crazy for you, princess." I pick her up by the waist and sit her on the desk. "What are you wearing under this pretty dress today?" I push the hem up, sliding my hands along her thighs. I hit the garter belt and my dick punches out, painfully constricted in my pants.

"Hang on, bossman." She works the button on my cargo pants. "I might have a bit of the *blowing the boss* fantasy."

I groan and help her with my zipper, freeing my erection.

She slides off the desk and holds my gaze as she lowers to her knees.

I growl the moment she takes hold of the base of my

cock and stretches it to her lips. She flicks her tongue over my weeping slit, moaning.

I fist her hair then release it and massage her scalp then pull it taut again as she parts her lips and takes my length into her mouth. "Fuck, yeah, baby. That's so hot."

"Sir, I wanted to talk to you about my raise," she play-acts, batting her long lashes when she comes off my dick.

I grip her hair again and push my cock between her lips. "Let's see how your next performance review goes." My voice is pure gravel.

She takes me deep into the back of her throat, using her tongue to swirl the underside each time she pulls back.

I groan and growl, my breath quick and ragged.

She massages my balls and twists her hand around the base of my cock. I'm going to come any second now. It's too good. But I need to get her off. And the pot's still on the stove.

"Enough," I grit out in that bossy tone she loves to hate. "I need you on my desk. Now."

She laughs and pops off my cock, letting me lift her to standing, then onto the desk. I shove her back, my movements shaky and urgent. I rip her panties down her legs. My hungry mouth comes to her core. I'm too far gone to give her much finesse, but I suck with an urgency that makes her thighs clamp my ears and her nails score my shoulders.

Her eyes roll back in her head with the pleasure of it, but she pushes me away. "Give me that big, bossy cock."

"Oh, I'll give it to you." I wrap an arm behind her hips to pull her right to the edge of the desk and line my cock up with her entrance. In one thrust, I'm inside her, moving in a way that feels life-affirming. Necessary.

I've claimed her, but I still can't ever get enough. She's

so perfect. My forever. My fate. My everything. It still feels like a miracle.

The desk slides over the floor as I pound into her, but I keep her cushioned by my arm, protected, as always. Her head falls back, eyes close. Her lips part for the desperate cries falling from her mouth.

We climax together, my lips on her throat, her legs behind my back.

"I love you, Rafe."

"I know, baby." I ease out and grab a few tissues to clean her up.

She smacks my shoulder.

"I love you too," I add, retrieving her silk panties and helping her back into them. "I need you. And you need me. We need each other." I straighten her clothes then mine.

She wraps her arms around my waist and places her head on my chest. "You gave up your revenge for me."

"Not quite," I draw back.

"Rafe, what is it? Is something wrong?" She gulps. "Is it Dieter?"

"No. He's in the wind. We don't know where he is, but he sold the mansion, so I don't think he's going to stick around or come after us."

She blows out a breath. "So he was telling the truth when he said he relinquished all rights to me."

"Looks like it." Arrogant fucker. He's still out there. But he made good on his word and let me take back Adele.

And then he sent us a packet of information—the second half of the file that he left at the cartel fire. Names and headshots of the men who took our parents plus a list of dates. Lance and I had Kylie check into it, and it turns out all the men were part of Data X. The dates in Dieter's file—the dates of their death?

I tell this to Adele.

"What's Data X?" she asks.

"A now defunct operation that was grabbing shifters. Data X doesn't exist anymore, but they were behind the attack. The men who came after my family wanted Lance and me. Our parents died for us."

"I'm so sorry, baby."

"It's okay." We've been grieving for years now. Decades. And now I have some closure. Data X has been shut down a long time, destroyed by shifters led by a brave lion–Nash Armstrong.

What's done is done. It's time for me to start a new life and a new family.

I'm meeting Adele's family at Mardi Gras, and if all goes well, I'll put a ring on it by Valentine's day. And in a few years, who knows? If Adele's willing, we'll give Lance's pup some cousins.

I dip my head and brush Adele's lips. She surges up to her tiptoes, giving herself to me. Her kisses are balm.

A bright ringing sound makes me throw open the door to see Channing walk by. He's got an elf hat on his head and ridiculous red slippers with bells on the tips. The ladies think he's cute, but the bells are obnoxious as fuck. Any second now Deke is going to tackle Channing and rip his slippers apart.

"Hey, Sarge, your phone is blowing up. You left it in the office. Figured you'd want to know" He hands it over, and the missed call is on the screen–Colonel Johnson.

"You take that. I need to check on the ham," Adele says.

I kiss her cheek and watch her curvy backside before heading to my office.

The colonel answers on the first ring. "Hello, son. Happy holidays," he barks.

"Same to you, sir."

"I hate to interrupt the festivities, but I got new intel on Dieter."

I tense and turn away from the open door. "Is he back in Taos?"

"Nope, far from it. He sold his Taos place. He's definitely not in town. But his behavior got me thinking."

"You mean his twisted fucking games? That behavior?"

"Exactly. I didn't get what he was doing, but it got me looking at what we do know: he's wealthy. Reclusive. Builds a private army. Collects treasures."

"Don't forget, *plays games with his enemies*," I add in a bitter tone.

"Exactly. Plus, he has inside knowledge about mates and shifters."

"What are you saying sir? Dieter's a shifter?"

"All signs point to him being one. The question is, what type? But then there was that last bit of intel you gave me. It was in Utah, right before you challenged him as a wolf. You told me about his eyes. The golden color. The slitted pupil. He could be a cat shifter, but the rest of it doesn't add up. There's only one creature that makes sense."

"Fuck me," I breathe, putting it together, just as Colonel Johnson says, "I think I know what Dieter is…"

EPILOGUE

Tabitha

"Come on, come on," I coax my ancient VW bus up the mountain road. It bounces over the unpaved dirt and rocks.

I check my phone for the thousandth time, but I've still got no service. Luckily I printed off directions to the estate sale. Whoever decided to build their mansion way out here in the Sangre de Cristo mountains was ridiculous, but they're not the first rich person to want their privacy.

Finally my bus reaches the top of the road and comes into a flat, empty clearing. I circle around it slowly, but it's the end of the road. What the heck? I'm in the middle of nowhere.

I check my directions. Guess I did take a wrong turn. If I'm at the correct address, there's nothing here but a big clearing.

So much for this estate sale. It was a private invite on one of the apps I follow, but I checked it out, and it seemed legit. There were droolworthy pictures of antique jewelry—garnets and agate and turquoise—dating back to the

189

Ottoman Sultans, verified by an auction company and everything. I already had a buyer lined up for one of the brooches.

Oh well. My map service had a satellite view of a fancy Tudor house at this location. Unless that sagebrush is hiding a mansion, the satellite view was wrong.

I get out of the car to stretch my legs. I've been driving for hours, and the last living thing I saw was some buzzards picking at roadkill twenty miles back.

My pink bus is streaked with red dirt. I shake out my skirt and do a few lunges around the clearing. A few more yoga poses to stretch my lower back, and I'll hit the road. I have just enough gas to get me back onto the highway and to a station.

I'm stretching my arms overhead when my skin prickles. I'm alone here, but my instincts are going nuts, telling me that someone else is here. But where?

I spin in a slow circle. A large shadow creeps over the desert, headed my way. Must be a plane or something but when I look up, I don't see anything. *Weird.*

The wind picks up, blowing grit into my face. I shade my eyes, but it's like someone turned a huge fan on above me. My hair whips back in the sudden gust, and my peasant skirt molds to my legs.

The shadow has almost reached me. For a moment, it looks like a pair of outstretched wings. And then a huge shape glides over me, blocking out the sun...

Coming soon: *Alpha's Fire*: starring Tabitha & Gabriel Dieter

WANT MORE?

Alpha's Fire

I've waited 1000 years for my mate. If she rejects me, I'll burn down the world.

She woke the dragon.

Every maiden dreams of being rescued by a handsome prince from a deadly dragon. But I'm both prince and dragon.

Ancient courtship rituals demand I steal my bride away. Imprison her in my high tower. Show her my treasures, my vast lands and armies.

I've done all that, and she still refuses me. She says she can't see herself with a man who still thinks Istanbul is Constantinople.

I must woo her, and I don't know how. But beneath my beating human heart, a dragon sleeps. And when he wakes, no one can stop him from destroying the world.

No one but *her*.

WANT FREE BOOKS?

Go to http://subscribepage.com/alphastemp to sign up for Renee Rose's newsletter and receive a free books. In addition to the free stories, you will also get special pricing, exclusive previews and news of new releases.

Download a free Lee Savino book from www.leesavino.com

OTHER TITLES BY RENEE ROSE

Hollywood Daddy

Stepbrother Daddy

Master Me Series

Her Royal Master

Her Russian Master

Her Marine Master

Yes, Doctor

Double Doms Series

Theirs to Punish

Theirs to Protect

Holiday Feel-Good

Scoring with Santa

Saved

Other Contemporary

Black Light: Valentine Roulette

Black Light: Roulette Redux

Black Light: Celebrity Roulette

Black Light: Roulette War

Black Light: Roulette Rematch

Punishing Portia (written as Darling Adams)

The Professor's Girl

Safe in his Arms

Paranormal

Two Marks Series

Untamed

Tempted

Desired

Enticed

Wolf Ranch Series

Rough

Wild

Feral

Savage

Fierce

Ruthless

Wolf Ridge High Series

Alpha Bully

Alpha Knight

Bad Boy Alphas Series

Alpha's Temptation

Alpha's Danger

Alpha's Prize

Alpha's Challenge

Alpha's Obsession

Alpha's Desire

Alpha's War

Alpha's Mission

Alpha's Bane

Alpha's Secret

Alpha's Prey

Alpha's Sun

Shifter Ops

Alpha's Moon

Alpha's Vow

Alpha's Revenge

Midnight Doms

Alpha's Blood

His Captive Mortal

All Souls Night

Alpha Doms Series

The Alpha's Hunger

The Alpha's Promise

The Alpha's Punishment

The Alpha's Protection (Dirty Daddies)

Other Paranormal

The Winter Storm: An Ever After Chronicle

Sci-Fi

Zandian Masters Series

His Human Slave

His Human Prisoner

Training His Human

His Human Rebel

His Human Vessel

ALSO BY LEE SAVINO

Paranormal romance

The Berserker Saga and Berserker Brides (menage werewolves)

These fierce warriors will stop at nothing to claim their mates.

Draekons (Dragons in Exile) with Lili Zander (menage alien dragons)

Crashed spaceship. Prison planet. Two big, hulking, bronzed aliens who turn into dragons. The best part? The dragons insist I'm their mate.

Bad Boy Alphas with Renee Rose (bad boy werewolves)

Never ever date a werewolf.

Tsenturion Masters with Golden Angel

Who knew my e-reader was a portal to another galaxy? Now I'm stuck with a fierce alien commander who wants to claim me as his own.

Contemporary Romance

Royal Bad Boy

I'm not falling in love with my arrogant, annoying, sex god boss. Nope. No way.

Royally Fake Fiancé

The Duke of New Arcadia has an image problem only a fiancé can fix. And I'm the lucky lady he's chosen to play Cinderella.

Beauty & The Lumberjacks

After this logging season, I'm giving up sex. For…reasons.

Her Marine Daddy

My hot Marine hero wants me to call him daddy…

Her Dueling Daddies

Two daddies are better than one.

Innocence: dark mafia romance with Stasia Black

I'm the king of the criminal underworld. I always get what I want. And she is my obsession.

Beauty's Beast: a dark romance with Stasia Black

Years ago, Daphne's father stole from me. Now it's time for her to pay her family's debt…with her body.

ABOUT RENEE ROSE

USA TODAY BESTSELLING AUTHOR RENEE ROSE loves a dominant, dirty-talking alpha hero! She's sold over a million copies of steamy romance with varying levels of kink. Her books have been featured in USA Today's *Happily Ever After* and *Popsugar*. Named Eroticon USA's Next Top Erotic Author in 2013, she has also won *Spunky and Sassy's* Favorite Sci-Fi and Anthology author, *The Romance Reviews* Best Historical Romance, and has hit the *USA Today* list ten times with her Bad Boy Alphas, Chicago Bratva, and Wolf Ranch series.

Renee loves to connect with readers!
www.reneeroseromance.com
reneeroseauthor@gmail.com

ABOUT LEE SAVINO

Lee Savino is a USA today bestselling author, mom and chocoholic.

Warning: Do not read her Berserker series, or you will be addicted to the huge, dominant warriors who will stop at nothing to claim their mates.

I repeat: Do. Not. Read. The Berserker Saga.

Download a free book from www.leesavino.com (don't read that either. Too much hot, sexy lovin').

Printed in Great Britain
by Amazon